"Stop!"

Heads turned sharply to see the man who'd called out. He stood there in a shaft of sunlight, head up, arms akimbo, his face wearing a challenging grin. Kaye held her breath, her heart beating fast, not daring to believe that Jack had come into her life, when she'd given up hope.

He strode down the aisle. "I have a prior claim on this woman," he declared. "Until that's satisfied, she can't marry anyone." With that, Jack seized Kaye up into his arms, and before she knew it they were in the church courtyard.

"You can't do things like that," Kaye gasped.

"I *can*," Jack said confidently. "Besides, I *do* have a prior claim on you. Had you forgotten?"

"No. I said I'd do anything you asked, whenever you asked."

"Anything, any time, any place. That was your promise. And now I've come to collect."

Dear Reader,

February is the month of love…glorious love. And to commemorate the soul-searching connection between a man and a woman, Special Edition has six irresistibly romantic stories that will leave you feeling warm and toasty from the inside out.

Patricia Thayer returns to Special Edition with *Baby, Our Baby!*—a poignant THAT'S MY BABY! tale that promises to tug the heartstrings. Ali Pierce had one exquisite night with the man she adored, and their passionate joining brought them the most precious gift of all—a child. You won't want to miss this deeply stirring reunion romance about the tender bonds of family.

Cupid casts a magical spell over these next three couples. First, an intense bodyguard falls for the feisty innocent he's bound to protect in *The President's Daughter* by award-winning author Annette Broadrick. Next, *Anything, Any Time, Any Place* by Lucy Gordon is about a loyal bride who was about to marry her groom, until a mesmerizing man insisting he had a prior claim on her heart whisks her away…. And a forbidden desire is reignited between a lovely librarian and a dashing pilot in *The Major and the Librarian* by Nikki Benjamin.

Rounding off the month, celebrated author Robin Lee Hatcher debuts in Special Edition with a compelling story about a man, a woman and the child that brings them together—this time forever—in *Hometown Girl*. And finally, *Unexpected Family* by Laurie Campbell is a heartfelt tale about a shocking secret that ultimately brings one family closer together.

I hope you enjoy all our captivating stories this month. Happy Valentine's Day!

Sincerely,

Karen Taylor Richman
Senior Editor

Please address questions and book requests to:
Silhouette Reader Service
U.S.: 3010 Walden Ave., P.O. Box 1325, Buffalo, NY 14269
Canadian: P.O. Box 609, Fort Erie, Ont. L2A 5X3

LUCY GORDON

ANYTHING, ANY TIME, ANY PLACE

Silhouette®

SPECIAL EDITION®

Published by Silhouette Books

America's Publisher of Contemporary Romance

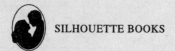

SILHOUETTE BOOKS

ISBN 0-373-24227-1

ANYTHING, ANY TIME, ANY PLACE

Copyright © 1999 by Lucy Gordon

Printed in U.S.A.

Books by Lucy Gordon

Silhouette Special Edition

Legacy of Fire #148
Enchantment in Venice #185
Bought Woman #547
Outcast Woman #749
Seduced by Innocence #902
Forgotten Fiancée #1112
Anything, Any Time, Any Place #1227

Silhouette Romance

The Carrister Pride #306
Island of Dreams #353
Virtue and Vice #390
Once Upon a Time #420
A Pearl Beyond Price #503
Golden Boy #524
A Night of Passion #596
A Woman of Spirit #611
A True Marriage #639
Song of the Lorelei #754
Heaven and Earth #904
Instant Father #952
This Man and This Woman #1079

Silhouette Desire

Take All Myself #164
The Judgement of Paris #179
A Coldhearted Man #245
*My Only Love, My
    Only Hate* #317
A Fragile Beauty #333
Just Good Friends #363
Eagle's Prey #380
For Love Alone #416
Vengeance Is Mine #493
Convicted of Love #544
The Sicilian #627
On His Honor #669
Married in Haste #777
Uncaged #864
Two Faced Woman #953
This Is My Child #982

LUCY GORDON

met her husband-to-be in Venice, fell in love the first evening and got engaged two days later. They're still happily married and now live in England with their three dogs. For twelve years Lucy was a writer for an English women's magazine. She interviewed many of the world's most interesting men, including Warren Beatty, Richard Chamberlain, Sir Roger Moore, Sir Alec Guinness and Sir John Gielgud.

In 1985 she won the *Romantic Times* Reviewers' Choice Award for Outstanding Series Romance Author. She has also won a Golden Leaf Award from the New Jersey Chapter of RWA, was a finalist in the RWA Golden Medallion contest in 1988 and won the 1990 RITA Award in the Best Traditional Romance category for *Song of the Lorelei*.

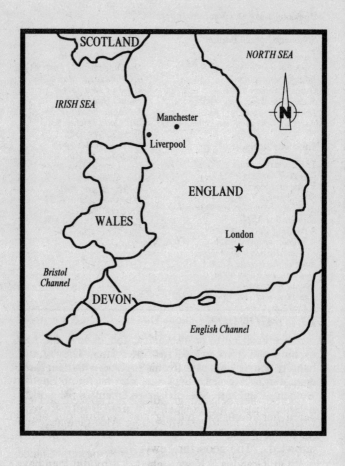

Prologue

Kaye's wedding dress was grandiose, with yards of embroidered satin sweeping the floor, and seed pearls adorning the tight bodice. Diamonds sparkled about her throat and on her ears. Her groom had insisted on it. He wanted the world to see that he was a rich man who'd bought and paid for his bride, even though she hated him.

Bertie, her beloved grandfather, knocked and entered her room, fat, puffing and bursting out of his wedding togs. ''You look lovely, darling,'' he growled. ''Too good for Lewis Vane.''

''Oh, Grandpa.'' Kaye sighed. ''Why did Paul have to steal from Lewis?''

''Because your mother raised him to think he could do as he liked,'' Bertie said angrily. ''And now you're being sacrificed to get him out of a mess of his own making. You should have refused to marry Lewis.''

"How could I when he could send Paul to prison? He'd do it, too. He's got all that evidence."

"A spell in jail would do your brother good," Bertie said bluntly. "Kaye, darling, if only you'd learn to stand up for yourself! Your father wouldn't have allowed this."

Kaye's father had been Bertie's son. When Kaye was six, Rhoda, her mother, had left home for another man, leaving her daughter behind. There'd been a divorce, a remarriage, and Paul had been born. It was only when her father died that Kaye had gone to live with Rhoda. Her mother had never loved her very much. Now Paul was the center of her world, and Kaye was expected to help look after him.

She'd adored her pretty little brother. Her nature was gentle and yielding, and she was too warmhearted to be jealous. It was Rhoda's new husband who minded never having his wife's attention, who had walked out.

As Paul grew up, Kaye was his protector, always getting him out of the trouble he'd brought on himself. Now here she was, on her wedding day, about to do so again.

She stood up to brush Bertie's coat. To do so she had to set down something she was holding in her hand. It was a tiny wooden ornament in the shape of a horse.

"I didn't know you'd kept Jack's present," Bertie said gently. "He meant a lot to you, didn't he?"

"Yes," she said softly. "Jack meant everything to me. But it was all a long time ago, and—and I didn't mean anything to him."

For a moment her eyes were hazy with longing at

the thought of the bright dream that would finally die today. Bertie put his arms about her and they clung together.

"You go down first," she said at last. "I'll follow soon."

She needed a moment alone, even from Bertie. Just one last moment to say a whispered goodbye to the man she had secretly loved for six years.

Jack Masefield.

She said his name softly, longingly, using the sound of the words to conjure up the big, laughing bear of a man who'd won her heart in the first moment.

She'd known him for just ten days, and they'd been the happiest of her life. He'd given her the little horse, but he'd also given her a flowering joy that she would never forget.

They'd parted so suddenly that she'd felt as though her heart had been torn out. She'd made him a promise, hoping that one day he would come back and claim it.

But he never had. And now he never would.

Bertie sat beside her in the car and held her hand comfortingly all the way to the church.

"I'll be all right, Grandpa," she said with a smile. "Honestly I will."

"You always said that when you were hurt, darling," he told her sadly. "As a child, when you fell over, you'd never cry."

"And I won't cry today," she promised him.

At the church she took his arm and began the march down the aisle with her head up. The altar grew inexorably nearer, with Lewis standing there, looking smug at having acquired her at last. Kaye's heart sank at the thought of spending her life with this spiteful man.

The parson began the wedding service, taking Kaye step by step to her doom. She heard the words, "If any of you know just cause or impediment why these persons may not be joined together, let him speak now, or forever hold his peace."

He'd already taken a breath to continue when a voice came ringing from the back of the church.

"Stop! There is an impediment."

Heads turned sharply to see the man who'd called out. He stood there in a shaft of sunlight, tall and straight, head up, arms akimbo, his face wearing a challenging grin. Kaye held her breath, her heart beating fast, not daring to believe that this man had come back into her life when she'd given up hope.

He strode down the aisle. "I have a prior claim on this woman," he declared. "Until that's satisfied, she can't marry anyone."

"Jack," Kaye whispered. "Jack Masefield."

Nobody heard her. A buzz was going around the church. Lewis Vane glared at the parson.

"Get on with it," he muttered.

"I must ask some questions first," the little man protested. "You mentioned a prior claim, sir. Do you mean that this lady is your wife?"

"No, but she's under an obligation to me." Jack Masefield's eyes were fixed on Kaye's face.

"Damned nonsense!" Lewis Vane roared. "Get out of here now."

"Certainly."

Jack made a half turn as if to leave, but at the last moment he swiveled around and seized Kaye up into his arms. Before anyone realized what was happening he was halfway out of the church with her.

A gleaming car stood outside, with a man at the wheel, the engine running and the rear door wide open. Jack set Kaye down in the back, slammed the door behind them and called, ''Move it!''

The next moment they were out of the churchyard, speeding away. Through the rear window Kaye saw a stream of guests pour out of the church. In the lead was Lewis Vane, red faced and bellowing, with Paul beside him looking horrified, and Rhoda screaming hysterically. Bertie was dancing with glee, waving his arms and yelling, *''Ye-es!''*

Perhaps one minute had elapsed since Jack had entered the church, and in that time the world had turned upside down.

''You can't do things like that!'' Kaye gasped.

''*I* can,'' Jack said with his self-confident grin. ''Besides, I *do* have a prior claim on you. Six years ago you gave me a promise. Had you forgotten?''

''No. I said I'd do anything you asked, whenever you asked.''

''Anything, any time, any place,'' he confirmed. ''That was your promise. And now I've come to collect.''

Chapter One

Bertie was a contest freak. He entered everything, yet had never won so much as a booby prize until the day, six years ago, when he'd scooped a holiday for two on the little Caribbean island of Singleton.

Kaye had just passed her eighteenth birthday, and he'd taken her with him, ignoring hints from Rhoda that Paul was looking peaked. It seemed the fates were making up to Bertie for years of disappointment. The contest organizers flew them out first class, put them up in a luxury hotel and provided generous spending money.

"Do you realize...." Bertie chuckled as they relaxed by the pool on their first day. "This hotel is filled with superrich folk, and we're living as if we belonged with them."

"Mmm!" Kaye stretched luxuriously on her reclining bed. "Is this really happening?"

Bertie frowned at her modest one-piece swimsuit. "You've got to get a bikini like all the others." He indicated the voluptuous females reclining around the pool. "That thing makes you look like a schoolgirl."

"But I've got a figure like a schoolgirl." She sighed. "I don't go in and out in the right places. Not enough, anyway—*hey!*"

The yell was forced from her by a large air-filled ball landing on her stomach. Kaye sat up indignantly and found herself looking into a pair of piercing blue eyes, set in the small, determined face of a little girl of about eight.

"That's my ball," she said.

"And that's my tummy it landed on," Kaye said.

"I didn't mean it to."

"Glad to hear it."

"I was aiming at him." The child indicated Bertie. "'Cos he's got a *much* bigger tummy than you."

Bertie regarded his bulge. "Guess I do make a tempting target."

"That's not the point," Kaye said, laughing. "You shouldn't chuck balls at people."

"But I'm a free spirit," the child explained. "Mommy says free spirits aren't bound by ordinary rules."

"That sounds very convenient," Kaye said thoughtfully. "So if I were a free spirit, I could puncture this ball."

"No, you couldn't, because it's mine."

"But I'm a free spirit, not bound by ordinary rules," Kaye pointed out.

The little girl opened her mouth, then closed it again, obviously taken aback by this view of things.

''Well,'' she said reluctantly at last, ''I guess you need *some* rules.''

·''*Georgy!* Cut it out!''

A man wearing only a pair of black shorts caught up with the little girl and admonished her in a voice that was half laughing, half harassed. Kaye looked up at him and felt her heart miss a beat.

He was a good six feet four inches, with broad shoulders, long, muscular legs, a flat stomach and powerful torso dusted with curly hair. But it wasn't his body's magnificence that took her breath away. It was his generous mouth with its smile of sheer devilment, as though the whole world were his to be relished.

He looked vaguely familiar, but then Kaye realized that her heart had known him all her life. And would know him forever. It had happened in one moment.

''I'm afraid my daughter's a bit out of hand,'' he said ruefully. ''I hope she didn't hurt you.''

''Not a bit,'' Kaye said, smiling.

''And I apologize for what she said about you, sir.''

''Forget it,'' Bertie said amiably.

''I want my ball,'' the child said.

''How about some manners, young lady?'' the man demanded.

''Can I have my ball back, please?''

Kaye handed it over and Georgy skipped away. The man gave a wry look and sat down beside Kaye's recliner.

''I'm Jack Masefield,'' he said, offering his hand.

His name, too, struck a chord, but Kaye hardly noticed. She was absorbed in his overwhelming presence.

His handshake was like the rest of him, huge and warm. Her small hand vanished without trace.

When they had swapped names Jack hailed a passing waiter to order drinks. Kaye chose something long and cold, and the men had beers.

"I'm afraid I make a poor hand at being a father," Jack admitted. "Georgy lives with my ex-wife most of the time and, as you saw, does pretty much as she likes."

His eyes were the same deep blue as Georgy's. Kaye hoped he hadn't noticed her little start of pleasure at the discovery that his wife was "ex."

"I haven't seen you around before," Jack observed, smiling at her.

It was a friendly rather than a flirtatious smile, but it turned her to jelly. Suddenly Kaye was hot and cold all over, desperately conscious of her dowdy swimsuit, and determined to buy a bikini as soon as possible.

Bertie explained that they'd arrived only the night before and had a suite on the second floor, but he said nothing about the competition. Jack was left to assume that they were millionaires exploring the world's playgrounds. Kaye turned an aghast look on Bertie, but he refused to meet her eyes.

"What line are you in, sir?" Jack asked respectfully.

"The gift trade," Bertie declared with truth, having spent his working life behind the counter of a fancy goods shop.

"I do a little of that myself," Jack said. "I'm in sports goods, but it crosses the line into gifts."

Kaye couldn't follow much of the talk that followed, but at first Bertie held his own. When he started to flounder help came unexpectedly.

"Jack! Phone!" A tall, thin man was coming around the side of the pool, waving to him.

"Thanks, Sam!" Jack gave them a friendly salute and moved off.

"Sam Masefield," the man declared, holding out his hand. "I'm Jack's father." He sat down beside them, stretched his arms and took deep breaths. "Perfect weather for action."

"What kind of action?" Bertie asked.

"Boating, hang gliding. I'm taking out a jet ski today. We sell them, and I test them out to make sure they're 'safe for all ages.' That's our marketing slogan."

"Sports goods!" Kaye said suddenly. "Of course! Masefield & Masefield."

"That's us," Sam declared.

M&M dominated the world of sports and leisure. Their stores were everywhere, selling excellent merchandise at reasonable prices.

"Did you say jet ski?" Bertie asked, his eyes gleaming.

"Ever tried one?"

"Nope."

"Want to?"

"Yup."

"Half an hour. See you on the beach."

Kaye went to the beach with Bertie at the allotted time and saw him mount a jet ski under Sam's dubious protection. Her anguished plea, "Do be careful, Grandpa," was answered with a lofty "Silence, woman!'' before he bounced away on his machine, clinging on for dear life.

She strolled back to the hotel's shopping mall, trying to get her bearings in a new world. Only an hour ago she hadn't met Jack Masefield, but now nothing would ever be the same again. His splendid frame, his dancing eyes and infectious smile were all a part of her, as completely as if she'd known him forever.

The bikini she chose showed off her delicate contours in a way that made her blush. Jack had come back and was talking to friends when she returned to the pool. Kaye stretched out in the sun, her fingers crossed, and at last her patience was rewarded.

''Georgy wants to say something to you,'' he said, drawing his daughter forward.

''I'm sorry for being cheeky,'' Georgy said reluctantly. She gave Kaye a smile that was just like her father's. ''And you look smashing in that bikini.''

''She's right about that,'' Jack confirmed, adding a soft, admiring whistle. Kaye was in seventh heaven.

When Georgy dropped her airs she was delightful. Kaye had a gift for getting on with children, and in a few minutes they were chatting easily while Jack looked on with pleasure. After Georgy had dashed off to play with some other children he said, ''I don't know how to thank you. I haven't seen her so happy since we started this vacation. I pinned so many hopes on it, but so far it hasn't worked out. I guess I don't know her well enough.''

''You don't see her very often?'' Kaye asked cautiously.

''Since our divorce Elsie and I mostly live in different countries. I see Georgy whenever I can, but she's a shrewd little monkey, and knows my weak spots."

"And you haven't—I mean, she doesn't have a stepmother to help you out?" Kaye asked, trying to sound casual, and hoping she wasn't blushing.

"No, I never married again," Jack said, and Kaye's world became brighter. "Too selfish, I guess. I like having my own way too much."

"I think you'd always manage to get your own way," Kaye said, trying to sound worldly-wise. "You're that kind of man."

He grinned. "That's just a highfalutin way of saying selfish. And I've already admitted that."

"I don't believe you're selfish," she said impulsively. Then, fearful that she'd sounded too fervent, she added in a teasing voice, "Self-indulgent, perhaps."

"Heaven help me! A woman who understands me!" he said in comic dismay. "Yes, I plead guilty to self-indulgence. And Georgy's my daughter. She didn't get it all from her mom."

"Poor little thing," Kaye murmured.

"Hey, I'm the one you should feel sorry for. She's in control, not me."

"Then she isn't happy. No child is happy being in control. Different countries! She doesn't know whether she's coming or going."

"Well, you've sure gotten on her right side. You handle her as well as Valerie. She's Georgy's nanny, a nice, reliable woman who gives the poor kid some stability. I thought she'd be coming on this trip, but at the last minute she decided to visit her sister instead. So I'm left to cope alone, and I'm floundering. Thank heavens for you! Look, would you and your grandfather have dinner with us tonight?''

"We'd love to," she said, her heart doing somersaults. "That is, if I ever see Grandpa again. Your father's taking him jet skiing."

"Don't worry. I always send a boat out after Sam at a discreet distance. If anything happens my captain has instructions to scoop him up."

"I think your father's wonderful," she said sincerely.

"Sam's great, isn't he? He spends his life doing things that turn my hair white."

"You seem to have inherited the gene. You're always in the papers, breaking speed or endurance records."

"Well, I can't let the old man have it all his own way. Besides, life gets dull behind a desk. What are your interests?"

"I swim a bit."

"Come and swim with me now." He held out his hand, and she took it eagerly.

He began to run through the trees to the nearby beach, drawing her with him. Ever afterward, that was one of her most poignant memories, her hand clasped safely in Jack's while she followed him gladly to a wonderful new world. He could light up the sky for everyone he met. Or perhaps she just thought so because she'd already fallen in love with him.

Jack had the whole top floor of the hotel, which accommodated not only Georgy and himself but Mrs. Mary Harris, his secretary, and Sam. Kaye soon learned that he traveled in a crowd wherever he went,

taking with him an atmosphere of cheerful unconcern
that was belied by the vision and drive with which he
ran his empire.

He needed to be active, and enjoyed testing new
equipment himself. He was funding the invention of a
new kind of hot air balloon, supposed to rise higher
and travel faster than any balloon before it. Jack had
accompanied the inventor on its maiden flight, and
their spectacular crash into the sea had made world
headlines.

The hotel had an outdoor nightclub on the beach,
and here Jack had a table large enough to accommo-
date his party. Kaye met Mary Harris and liked her at
once. She was middle-aged, shrewd and outspoken.
She shook Kaye's hand, taking in her appearance.
Kaye was sure Mary knew she'd bought the brightly
colored dress specially that afternoon, and that her
long hair had been done up for the occasion. And from
the kindly smile in the secretary's eye, she guessed
that she was just one in a long line of young women
competing for Jack's attention.

To her disappointment, she wasn't sitting beside
him, but she had a good view of him across the table.
On one side of her was Georgy, and on the other side
was a young man called Colin, who seemed bent on
paying her a lot of attention, until she began to feel
uncomfortable. Later he kept asking her to dance. She
was too inexperienced to get rid of him, until Jack
came to the rescue and edged him firmly out of the
picture.

"Thank you," Kaye said with relief. "He kept asking questions about Bertie's business until I didn't
know where to look."

"He was checking your finances. He needs a rich wife to save his father's firm."

"Jack, I've got to tell you. Grandpa isn't a tycoon, the way he implied. He won this vacation in a competition. We haven't got a bean."

Jack laughed so loud that several people turned to stare. He took her arm and drew her into the shadows. "What a wonderful old boy!" he exclaimed. "Good for him!"

"But we're frauds," she said.

"So be a fraud, and enjoy it. Life's too short to worry. Besides, everyone here is a fraud in one way or another. Some of them are about to go under, but they spend like mad to stop the world finding out."

"Oh, dear, there's Colin looking for me again. Do you think I should tell him the truth?"

"No need. I know a simpler way." Jack slipped an arm about her shoulders and drew her close. Colin read the message in that possessive gesture, and turned away.

"Now he'll think *you're* looking for a rich wife," Kaye said, laughing to cover the delicious tremors that were going through her.

"Don't worry. They all know me too well to think that," he said with a simplicity that went beyond arrogance. The next moment he caught sight of his daughter. "It's time you were in bed."

"Another half hour," she pleaded.

"You said that an hour ago. Scoot."

Seeing a storm about to break, Kaye took swift action. "Jack, would you mind if I borrowed Georgy for a while? I saw some scarves in the shop this afternoon and I'd like her opinion before I buy anything."

Georgy was ready to accept this compromise. Jack said, "And then you go to bed, okay?"

The shops in the mall stayed open until two in the morning. Kaye and Georgy spent a cheerful half hour going through the stock, before Kaye settled on something that was just within her budget.

"And that one," Georgy said, pointing at a luxurious scarf Kaye had admired. "Put it on my dad's card."

When they reached her room Georgy wrapped the scarf around Kaye's shoulders. "It's for you."

"Georgy, I can't take this! It's much too expensive."

Hastily she explained about the competition. Like her father, Georgy was entertained. "No problem. Dad'll pay."

"No way. What will he say if I let you buy me expensive gifts and simply charge them to him?"

"He'll say it's no big deal. I get what I like at that shop. Anyway, I want to give you something. You're okay. Dad treats me like a little girl, but you can handle him."

Kaye was left bereft of words. Having hinted at the bargain she expected, Georgy went to bed without further trouble, leaving Kaye to return to the beach with the silk scarf tied around her shoulders.

Jack was dancing. His partner was dark haired, lavishly beautiful and well endowed. Soon her place was taken by another woman out of the same mold. Jack danced cheek-to-cheek, whispering words that made his partners laugh or meet his eyes significantly. The sight made Kaye's heart ache, but she couldn't tear her gaze away.

At last he noticed her and stretched out his hand. Now, she thought, he would hold her close, but the band was playing a swinging calypso, in which they twisted and whirled and seldom touched.

Afterward she hastily explained about the scarf. As Georgy had predicted, he was relaxed. "You got that little monkey's mind off her tantrum and I'm grateful. She's got good taste, hasn't she? Those soft colors are perfect with your gray eyes."

"You can't see my eyes in this light," she protested.

"I saw them earlier. I remember them."

As flirtations went it was the mildest possible remark, but she blushed all over, glad of the darkness that hid her gaucheness.

The last dance was a waltz, and to her joy he danced it with her. It was disappointing that he didn't hold her close against him, but at least she was in his arms, savoring the warmth from his big body, looking up eagerly to meet his smile.

"You shouldn't look at a man like that," he teased. "It's dangerous."

She tried to think of a sophisticated reply, but the music was coming to an end. The most glorious day of her life was over.

"I'll walk you back," he said, slipping an arm about her shoulders.

The walk through the trees was magic. He didn't try to kiss her, but she was close to him, and for the moment that was all she asked. Heaven seemed very close that night.

The days that followed were the happiest she'd ever known. The two families joined forces, with Sam and

Bertie indulging in riotous living, and Kaye gladly spending her time with Georgy. She liked the little girl, and besides, that way she could be with Jack.

The child adored her father and enjoyed nothing better than being with him. Kaye noted approvingly that he gave her all his attention—or as much as the constantly ringing telephone would allow.

Father and daughter loved each other, but they didn't understand each other, and Kaye created a bridge between them. Once he said, "I shouldn't take over your vacation like this."

"I'm fine," she said airily. "I'm going to be an infant teacher, so I'm practicing on Georgy."

"You'll be a great teacher," he said.

Jack might have been selfish, as he claimed, and he was certainly used to taking his pleasures as he pleased. But he wasn't self-centered. He made Kaye talk about herself, and listened with every sign of interest. Sam and Georgy joined in, asking questions, and it was clear that Jack's charm was a family trait, since all three generations of Masefields had it by the wagonload. Encouraged, Kaye brought out her family snapshots, which were mostly of Paul. He was fourteen then, free of the spots that plagued his contemporaries, and already showing astonishing good looks.

"Wow!" Georgy said, taking the picture. "He's real cute."

"What did you say?" Jack demanded sharply.

"I'm glad you admire him," Kaye said, frowning at Jack.

He relapsed into fulminating silence until Georgy had gone off to play with some friends, then said explosively, "Cute! She thinks a boy is cute! She's eight years old, for Pete's sake!"

"That's how they talk at eight these days," Kaye said.

"When I was eight I practically didn't know girls were a different sex," Jack said, aghast.

"Well, you've sure made up for it since!" Sam said ribaldly. "Kaye's right. Keep quiet and don't let Georgy see she can wind you up."

Kaye was enchanted at Jack's streak of puritanism regarding his daughter, which contrasted sharply with the hedonism of his own life. Wherever he went women's eyes followed him, and he wasn't shy about enjoying what was freely offered.

One extravagantly built lady tried to commandeer his attention during the day. Jack was happy for her to join the family party but earned Kaye's respect by resisting the siren's attempts to detach him from Georgy. After a while the beauty flounced off. In this way, it happened that Kaye spent more time with Jack than any other woman.

One day he said, "I want to buy you a present to thank you for all you've done for Georgy, and to remember me by."

I'll remember you always, she thought. There won't be a moment when you don't live with me, just as you are now. I'll keep every word, every smile, and I'll cherish them in my heart until the day I die.

Aloud she said, "I don't want presents, Jack."

"What's the matter?" he asked, struck by a constraint in her tone. "Have I offended you? I didn't mean to. It's just that I owe you so much, and I like to pay my debts."

He was a scrupulous man who dealt fairly with everyone, and then forgot them. She too would be forgotten when he'd settled his accounts. The urge to make him remember her was overwhelming.

"Take me to the Serenita," she said. "I've always wanted to eat there."

"I've never heard of it."

"It's a restaurant half a mile along the beach. It's only a tiny place. The others wouldn't like it, but I think I'd enjoy a meal there."

She dressed carefully that evening, choosing a silk chiffon dress that he'd once casually admired, and her eyes were bright with anticipation.

Although it was early, darkness had already fallen as they strolled along the beach together. The little restaurant stood at the edge of the sand, with tables under the stars. Colored lights hung from the palm trees, and the air was heavy with the scent of flowers.

Jack was the perfect dinner companion, making her laugh, giving her all his attention. He'd seen her shopping in the arcade that afternoon, loading herself up with gaudy shirts.

"They're for Paul," she explained when he asked.

"You'll have nothing left if you blow all your money on him."

"But he was so disappointed when Grandpa brought me instead of him. I wanted to get him something nice."

"You really love your brother, don't you?"

"Oh, yes. More than anyone in the world, except Grandpa, of course."

"Are they the only men you love?" he asked quizzically. "What about a boyfriend?"

She managed to say lightly, "Oh, I'm playing the field," but she was sure she was blushing all over.

"Wise woman," Jack said. "Never make big decisions before you're twenty-five."

"You did," she said impulsively.

"That's right, I married at twenty-one," he said. "Which is a crazy age for a man to marry. And I made another fool mistake. I threw my whole heart into it."

"But you have to, or it couldn't work," she said, puzzled.

"It didn't work anyway. It was too one-sided. But I learned my lesson. Always keep something back."

"That's a terrible lesson," she said earnestly. "I hope I never learn that. If you love someone it would have to be with your whole heart and soul, because if you don't give absolutely everything you're—you're simply not *entitled* to anything back."

The smile he gave her was full of tenderness. "How young you are," he said softly. "Only someone very young could have said that."

"No, Jack, honestly, it's got nothing to do with being young. It's what I truly believe. I couldn't live any other way."

"You couldn't," he agreed. "But I haven't got your generous nature."

"Why, how silly! You're the most generous person I know. You're always giving things to people."

"Is that generosity?" he mused. "I wonder sometimes if giving people things isn't really a way of giving them nothing."

"I don't know what you mean."

"I'm glad. I hope you never know. I'm not good news, Kaye. Not really."

She was so overwhelmed with emotion that she almost made him a declaration of love right then and there. Before she could do so he made a small, disgruntled sound.

"I don't know what's gotten into me. All this analytical talk! Usually I'd rather do anything than pick thoughts to pieces, especially my own. It's something to do with you. Those beautiful eyes of yours see too much."

Before she could recover from her pleasure enough to answer, a man came dancing up to their table with a tray loaded with cheap souvenirs.

"Oh, please, Jack, would you get me one?" Kaye asked eagerly. "As a memento of—of this restaurant."

The trinkets were made of carved wood. She chose a little wooden horse dangling on a chain, just small enough to fit into her pocket.

"Wait," she cried impulsively as the seller prepared to go. When he turned back she took an identical horse from the tray and paid for it.

"It's for you," she said to Jack. "It could be a key ring."

As she said the words she recalled his solid gold key ring and could have wept for her own clumsiness. But he smiled and took her gift warmly. "You don't have to give me anything, Kaye. But I'm glad you did."

They strolled back together along the beach. Jack slipped his arm about her shoulders and this time she dared to put her own arm around his waist. The brilliant moon covered the world with silver, and everything was quiet, save for the soft plashing of the tiny waves. Kaye tried to pretend that they were the only people in the whole world, and wished it could be so. She loved him with her whole heart.

"What are you looking at?" Jack asked, following her upward gaze.

"The stars. They all seem so strange."

"That's because we're seeing them from much farther south than usual."

They stopped and gazed up together. Kaye had worn her hair up, but the movement of his arm loosened the pins, and it all tumbled down. She turned her head and found him looking at her, and her heart beat wildly as she saw the sudden response in his face. How she'd longed to see it there, and now at last it had happened. He saw her as a woman. She felt him draw her closer, and the next moment she was in his arms.

"Kaye..." His murmur was half a protest, as though he'd sworn not to let this happen. But if so, he was possessed by a desire stronger than his will, for almost at once he began to kiss her with hungry urgency.

He was a man used to indulging every demand of his senses. When he drew her down to the sand he was following a well-worn path that would end in pleasure and satiety.

To Kaye they were making love. In her innocence she had no idea that he was doing something entirely different. She felt the rough hairs of Jack's chest against her bare breasts and gasped with the unfamiliar pleasure. She'd lived this moment before in her fevered dreams, but not once had it been as poignantly sweet as this. Everything she'd longed for was happening, and in another moment she would know the joy of complete union.

"Kaye—" Jack said hoarsely, with something like alarm in his voice.

"Yes—yes—" She kissed him repeatedly, too consumed by happiness to heed the doubting note in his voice. "Oh, my love, my love..."

"Kaye—don't..." he begged.

"But I love you—I love you—"

It was as though her words had touched a spring. With a groan Jack pulled back sharply. *"No!"* he shouted. *"I'm not going to do this!"*

He wrenched himself out of her arms. In one terrible moment Kaye became aware of everything: Jack's face, distraught, eyes wide with horror, her own breasts in the moonlight. She had exposed more than her body. Her own terrible words, *I love you—I love you*— seemed to hang in the air.

"Oh, God," she wept. Turning away, she hurriedly covered herself and scrambled to her feet.

"Kaye, wait!" She felt Jack's hand on her arm, but shook him off and fled. She wanted to die before she ever had to look him in the face again. Tears poured down her face as she raced along the beach, frantically trying to outrun the sound of Jack's voice and the searing knowledge of her own shame.

She felt his hand on her arm. *"Let me go!"* she screamed, struggling, but he held her.

"Kaye, please," he begged, managing to get both arms around her. "Please hear me out."

"I don't want to listen," she cried. "I know—"

"But you don't know," he said frantically. "Oh, please, darling, don't cry. I didn't want to hurt you.

That's why I—don't you see that I couldn't—? Hush, hush!'' He pulled her head against his shoulder. ''I couldn't treat you like the others. They're all the same—easy come, easy go. But you're different. You're special, precious.''

She couldn't answer. His words seemed to her only commonplace reassurance. She'd made herself and her love cheap for a man who cared nothing for her. She had no more strength to struggle. She could only yield to her grief and sob bitterly on his shoulder, while he hushed her gently.

''I should never have let things get so far,'' he murmured. ''I don't know what I was thinking of, but you're so sweet and delightful. I should have been more careful of you—try to forgive me, darling.''

''Don't call me darling,'' she sobbed. ''It's not true. It'll never be true.''

''It'll be true one day, with a man more worthy of you than me. I'm a selfish devil, or this wouldn't have happened. But you'll find a man who knows how to treat you, and you'll love him.''

''I'll never love anyone but you,'' she whispered.

He drew back a little and took her face between his hands. ''Yes, you will,'' he said. ''And he'll be the luckiest man alive. I envy him already. When you find him, remember I said that.''

He kissed her softly on the eyes and on the lips, and dried her face with his own clean handkerchief. There was nothing more to be said, so Kaye let him take her hand and lead her back along the beach. He talked as they went, lightly, trying to calm her. And when they came in sight of the hotel she managed to hold her head up high.

Soon they were among the other guests. Jack gave her hand a squeeze before letting her go, and she didn't see him again that evening. That night she went to sleep holding the little wooden horse he'd given her.

Next day he was gone. Mrs. Harris explained that he'd taken Georgy on an expedition to the other side of the island, and wouldn't be back until the evening. She knew he'd gone to escape her. She had embarrassed him.

Sam, too, was away, and Bertie moped without his boon companion. He seemed tired and out of sorts, and at dinner he ate very little.

Then just as the meal finished he collapsed with a massive heart attack.

The hotel staff acted smartly and in a few minutes Bertie was in an ambulance on his way to the hospital. It was an excellent place but small, serving a tiny population. The kindly staff stabilized Bertie's condition, while Kaye frantically explained that this wasn't Bertie's first attack.

"He was supposed to be careful, but he wouldn't—"

"He should be flown to the mainland as soon as possible," Dr. Bukin said. "We can provide a flying ambulance, but I'm afraid there's a big charge."

"We've got insurance," Kaye said at once.

Dr. Bukin called the insurance company, and her heart sank as she saw his face become tense.

"I'm afraid there's a problem," he said when he'd hung up. "Your grandfather never told them he'd had a heart attack before. It's given them the excuse to invalidate his insurance. They won't pay."

"Then I will," Kaye said frantically. "I'll pay anything."

He told her the amount and she paled. "It doesn't matter. I'll work all my life to pay it off—"

"I'm sorry, but we need the money up front. Look, talk to them yourself."

She tried, but the insurers were adamant. Dr. Bukin took the phone from her. "I want you to realize that your attitude is condemning this man to death," he snapped.

Kaye could hear the tinny voice mouthing something about "company policy." Unable to bear any more, she ran out of the room, down the corridor and into the hospital grounds. Hysterical sobs tore at her, and she ran blindly until she felt two strong arms seize her, and a comforting voice say, "*Kaye!* It's all right, it's me."

"Jack—oh, Jack—" She was shaking too much to speak.

"I just got back and heard about Bertie. Is he—?"

"He's going to die," she cried in despair. "He needs a flying ambulance, but the insurers won't pay."

"All right, calm down. C'mon now, don't cry. I'm going to make it all right."

"You can't do anything," she wept. "He's dying."

"Hey, nobody tells Jack Masefield that he can't do something," he said gently. "Let's go inside."

The insurance company hadn't budged, but Jack immediately took charge. "Get the ambulance out," he told Dr. Bukin. "It's all taken care of. Do you have a phone I can use?"

Kaye raced back to see Bertie. He was lying still, an oxygen mask on his face and tubes attached to his arms. She leaned down as close as she could and whispered, "It's going to be all right. Jack's taking care of us. Just hang in there. Oh, don't give up now, darling."

Jack was waiting for her downstairs.

"The ambulance will be ready in half an hour," he said. "I'll drive you to the hotel to pack your things, and bring you back here. You're going to Florida. They've got one of the best hospitals in the world."

"But Jack, it'll be a private hospital and we've no insurance now."

"Kaye, stop fretting. It's all arranged."

She was silenced, awed by his generosity.

At the hotel she packed Bertie's things, then her own, and tucked the little wooden horse into her pocket.

They reached the hospital to find the ambulance plane there, and Bertie already being taken on board. "Now you," Jack said.

Suddenly it dawned on her that this was a final goodbye. "Jack," she said hurriedly, seizing his hands, "I know I can never really pay you back, but I will."

"Kaye, forget it, please."

"I don't mean money. I mean, one day I'll do something that's as important to you as this is to me. Anything you want, whenever you want. It doesn't matter where I am or what I'm doing at the time."

"All right. It's a deal."

"I mean it, Jack. Anything, any time, any place. For you I'll drop everything, at a moment's notice. Remember that."

"I'll remember." His warm eyes met hers for a moment, then he kissed her cheek kindly. "Take care of yourself, Kaye."

"You too. And don't forget..."

"Anything, any time, any place," he repeated. "I'll count on it."

He helped her aboard. The door slammed and the next moment they were moving. The last thing she saw was Jack waving, with a movement that was big and bold, like the man himself.

In Florida an ambulance was waiting at the airport, and they were whisked away to a gleaming white hospital with all the latest equipment. There was even a room for Kaye, so that she could be with Bertie constantly. He'd stood the journey well, and by next morning his condition was looking more hopeful. In two weeks he'd recovered enough to return to England.

Jack called the hospital every day to check Bertie's progress, but only once did he speak to Kaye. She tried to thank him again, but he wouldn't let her finish.

"I'm in your debt about Georgy," he said quickly. "As long as Bertie is improving."

She could tell he was eager to end the call, so she said something polite and hung up. Jack was being kind and conscientious, but for him it was all over.

That had been six years ago, and since then she'd had no contact with him. To her disappointment she hadn't even grown into the kind of voluptuous beauty he liked. Her figure had filled out a little, but her charms would never be ample. Her face was lovely in a delicate, understated way, but she scorned her own looks because they weren't the kind that pleased Jack.

At first the memory of the night on the beach had

devastated her. She relived it again and again, the bit-tersweet joy of being with him, the agony of his re-jection. It took time and acquaintance with other men for her to see it in its true light.

She had boyfriends, too many, Bertie said, for she was searching for something she would never find again. Her relationships fizzled out quickly, since no man was allowed too close to the heart of her, and none ignited her senses as Jack had done. And when they discovered her physical coldness they reacted in ways she found illuminating. Mostly they behaved self-ishly, and by contrast she came to see Jack's action in its true light, as a generous man's most completely generous act.

She followed his exploits in the papers avidly, and couldn't help her heart beating faster at the sight of him with a curvaceous brunette on his arm.

The last time had been a month ago, when he'd crashed his speedboat at sea and ended up in the hos-pital for a stay that was expected to be two weeks but had actually been two days. He'd emerged determined to take the speedboat back to sea at the first chance. The newspaper had shown him with his arm about a young woman with long hair, who was looking up at him. Kaye couldn't see her face, but she could see Jack's. His eyes, as he gazed down at his companion, had been filled with a warmth that hadn't been there before.

Kaye understood that look. This was no longer a man playing the field, but a man who'd found some-one special. She knew she had no right to feel pain. But she did, nonetheless.

She could never be anything to Jack, but one day he might call in her promise. If only he would come back for her, she thought wistfully.

And then, on her wedding day, he did....

Chapter Two

"How could you do that?" Kaye gasped as they sped away from the church. "How could you—?"

"He just did it, sweetheart," the driver boomed over his shoulder. "Simple as that."

"Sam!" she cried, and he turned his head to grin. *"Watch the road!"* He turned back just in time to avoid a collision.

"You're mad, both of you," she cried.

"That's right, we haven't changed a bit," Jack assured her.

His smile was as wide and heart stopping as she remembered, and a tremor went through her as though the past six years had never been.

"Anything, any time, any place," he reminded her. "That was your promise, and I'm calling it in. I need you, Kaye. I've got Georgy with me full-time now.

Elsie was into booze and toyboys in a big way, and it was just no life for a fourteen-year-old girl. Trouble is, Georgy was having a good time, so she wasn't happy when I whisked her away.

"Then I remembered you and how well you got on with Georgy. If you're looking after her, I can have an easy mind."

She gaped, barely able to believe her ears. "And you kidnapped me from my wedding for that?"

"Well, you didn't want to get married."

"How did you know that?"

For a moment he seemed awkward. "Er—I surveyed the territory first," he said hastily. "Never mind that. You're well out of it."

"But I have to marry Lewis," Kaye said urgently. "My brother, Paul, worked for him, and Lewis caught him stealing. He threatened to prosecute, but if I marry him, Paul will be safe."

"Will he? Or will he be used as a weapon to bully you with whenever Vane feels in the mood? Never mind. The wedding's off. Step on it, Sam."

"There's no sign of them," Kaye said, glancing out of the rear window.

"Your groom knows where I live."

"You know Lewis Vane?"

But of course, Jack knew everyone. She looked at him in a daze. He was so big and handsome, so confident that the world would dance to his tune. And perhaps he was right. It was like a miracle to find herself with him again.

Six years had hardly changed him. There were a few more laughter lines, but they only made his face more attractive. He still had the lean, hard figure of an athlete, still radiated a charisma so strong that it was almost like an aura.

He grinned and took her hands in his. "Don't fret," he advised her. "It's all going to be taken care of. Give me a kiss for old times' sake!"

Still holding her hands, he kissed her lightly on the mouth, then smiled directly into her eyes. "Trust me?"

"Yes," she said breathlessly.

"Good." He turned back to the front, keeping one of her hands tucked between the two of his. She left it there contentedly. She didn't understand anything, but it didn't matter. Jack Masefield had come storming back into her life, and she didn't want to wake up, ever.

"Where are we going?" she asked at last.

"Maple Lodge. It's my home when I'm in London. It's a nice little place. I've got a good school for Georgy nearby. Except that she doesn't want to go. Elsie let her do as she liked."

He called forward to Sam, "Did you pass my instructions on to Mary?"

"Every last one. You'll find it all done."

The car was slowing to turn into a drive, and Kaye got her first glimpse of Jack's "nice little place." It was a mansion set in extensive grounds. Through some maple trees she glimpsed a swimming pool, then the trees cleared, revealing a large solid building with a roof of red tiles.

A beautiful young woman with long hair stood in the porch waiting, and Kaye's heart sank as she realized that this must be Jack's girlfriend, the one he'd been hugging in the newspaper picture. Then the young woman waved, and Kaye stared in recognition.

"*Georgy?*" she breathed.

"Georgy," Jack confirmed.

"Then you haven't—" She checked herself before she could blurt out *haven't got a girlfriend.*

"Haven't what?"

"Nothing," Kaye said hastily. "I'm just amazed. Georgy was only eight when I knew her—"

"And she's fourteen now, but she could pass for twenty. So she thinks she *is* twenty."

The girl ran forward to greet her, brimming over with excitement. To her this was obviously a thrilling game.

"Everything's ready," she told her father, taking Kaye's hand and drawing her indoors. Kaye followed, still in a daze from the wonderful thing she'd just discovered. Jack didn't have a girlfriend. The warmth she'd seen in his eyes in the picture had been a father's warmth. It was crazy to be so happy, and yet her joy spouted up to the ceiling like a wellspring.

The big front room bore several tables covered with white cloths and laden with food and champagne. "Just like a wedding feast," Jack said appreciatively.

"Because we're going to entertain a wedding party," Georgy finished triumphantly. Her laughter matched her father's, and their resemblance was very clear. She'd inherited his height, too, and was already taller than most women.

"Well, we've got the bride," Sam said, "and I reckon the guests will be here any moment."

A heavily built man was standing in the corner of

the room. Jack hailed him as Harry, but didn't introduce him.

"Here's an old friend you'll remember," he said as Mary came into the room.

The secretary was a little grayer, but her smile was as friendly as ever, and she embraced Kaye warmly. "It's lovely to see you again, and don't you worry. Everything's going to be all right."

Kaye gave her a puzzled look. Surely Mary couldn't know as much about her situation as her remark implied. Jack spoke quickly. "They're here!"

Looking out of the window, Kaye saw a stream of cars pouring up the drive to disgorge various disgruntled passengers.

"Leave the talking to me," Jack said.

"Gladly."

First into the room was Kaye's mother, Rhoda. She was overdressed, even for a wedding. On her shoulder she wore a ruby-and-diamond brooch, Lewis Vane's reward to her for bullying her daughter into the marriage, and a reminder of what she stood to lose if things went wrong. She still had the remains of good looks, but they were marred by spite and smugness.

She made straight for her daughter. "I don't know what you think you're playing at," she seethed, "but you get back to that church this minute."

"You're forgetting that I kidnapped her," Jack said. "And I'm going to insist that she stays here."

"*You!*" Rhoda turned on him. "Do you think I don't know she put you up to it?"

Paul had glided in behind his mother and stood there, poised and handsome, surveying his surroundings. His looks were of the classic, Adonis type, with a straight nose, high cheekbones, and large, dark eyes. There was a sweetness in his smile that made everyone his friend. The only flaw was a lack of resolution in his chin and the corners of his mouth, and that was less evident now than it might become later.

As he looked around him at the luxurious room, his lips pursed in a silent whistle, which was repeated as his gaze reached Georgy. The girl smiled appreciatively at his handsome face, and sashayed over.

"I'm Georgy," she said in a low voice.

"I'm Paul." He gave her his "never fail" smile.

Bertie and Sam greeted each other like long-lost brothers, with slaps on the back and sentimental yelps of delight. "Have a drink," Sam said.

"Wouldn't mind a drop of champagne, at that."

"Champagne? Pooh! Have a man's drink." He shoved a large tumbler of malt whiskey into Bertie's hand, and poured one for himself.

Lewis Vane entered aloofly, and his cold eyes hardened as they rested on Jack.

"Mom, I didn't put anyone up to anything," Kaye protested. "I didn't know Jack was coming."

"Nonsense!" Rhoda scoffed. "All that stuff about a prior claim."

"But that was true," Jack said mildly. "Kaye promised me six years ago that she was at my service whenever I liked. By the way, I don't think I have the pleasure of your acquaintance."

"This is my mother, Mrs. Benton," Kaye said, wanting to sink through the floor. "Mom, this is Jack Masefield. This is his father, Sam. Jack, this is my brother, Paul."

"Oh, so you do remember you've got a brother, do

you?'' Rhoda sneered. ''You can think of *someone* apart from yourself.''

''Mom, please...'' Kaye said in a desperate whisper.

''You know what this wedding means to your family,'' Rhoda snapped. ''But no, that's not good enough for you! Self, self, self! That's all you ever think of.''

''Come on, Mom,'' Paul said hastily. ''Let's not have a go at Kaye. It was just a misunderstanding.'' He squeezed Kaye's hand and gave her an appealing smile. ''We can still have the wedding.''

''I damned well hope so,'' Lewis Vane said sourly. ''I don't like being made to look a fool.'' He stepped up to Kaye. ''Get moving.''

''She's staying here,'' Jack said.

''No way,'' Vane snapped, with a significant glance at Paul, who flinched. ''There's a lot you don't know.''

''There's a lot I *do* know, Vane,'' Jack said quietly. ''Enough to spike your guns.''

''I'm not standing for this,'' Rhoda seethed. ''I haven't worn myself to a shred over this wedding just to see you ruin it.''

''But perhaps she doesn't want to get married,'' Jack suggested in a tone of deceptive mildness.

''Of course she does.'' Rhoda spat out the words. ''She's just playing her tricks.''

''Why don't we talk about it?'' Jack suggested smoothly.

''I'm not talking with some hired actor, or whatever you are,'' Rhoda said sharply.

Bertie had been muttering to Paul, putting him

straight on a few facts, and now the young man intervened quickly. "Leave it, Mom," he muttered.

"And who's going to save your bacon?" she snapped.

"He's not an actor, Mom," Paul said. "This is his home."

If there was one thing Rhoda could do, it was price goods to the penny. A rapid glance around showed her that she was in the presence of serious money, and she modified her tone, although only slightly. "If you weren't hired, who are you?" she demanded. "I don't know you."

"But your daughter does," Jack said, pressing a glass of champagne into her hand. "We met six years ago. I was able to help her when Bertie was taken ill."

"He saved my life," Bertie confirmed.

"He saved my pal's life," Sam agreed emotionally. Rhoda favored him with a look that would have struck him dead if he hadn't been refilling Bertie's glass.

"Kaye promised to repay the debt any time, and in any way I asked," Jack continued.

Rhoda sniffed. "I'll bet she did. I know your kind. No prizes for guessing what you want."

"Mom, please..." Kaye said wretchedly.

Jack glanced at her, puzzled. The girl he'd known on Singleton had been young and gentle, but strong. There'd been authority in the way she'd dealt with Georgy, as well as humor. Yet now she seemed helpless, caught in her mother's spite like an animal trapped in headlights.

When Rhoda paused to gulp some champagne he whispered in Kaye's ear, "Tell her to get lost. She can't eat you."

"She's my mother," Kaye said desperately.

Her groom had been watching her with cold dislike. Now he said, "I would like a word with you in private, Kaye."

Before she could move, Jack got between them. "No," he said simply.

"This is none of your damned business," Lewis raged.

"I'm making it my business. Kaye isn't marrying you."

"I think she is," Lewis said with a sneer. "I doubt she's told you everything."

"You've gotten a hold on her through her brother." Jack looked at Paul, biting his lip. "You young fool."

"It was a m-misunderstanding," Paul stammered.

"We'll let the police decide about that," Lewis said. "They'll be interested in what I'll tell them, especially in view of your criminal record."

"It—it was nothing," Paul said in answer to a raised eyebrow from Jack. "Just a bit of shoplifting."

"A criminal record is a criminal record," Vane said remorselessly. "Kaye! We're leaving, now!"

"She's not going," Jack said in a deceptively quiet voice.

"*Kaye,*" Paul said in an urgent whisper.

Jack set his glass down. There was only a small clinking noise, but it seemed to reverberate through the room like a roll of drums, announcing the drawing of battle lines. He looked Vane directly in the eyes.

"I said she's not going," he repeated.

"She'll regret it if she doesn't," Vane snapped.

"Not half as much as you'll regret it if she does. You want to play Blackmail? Okay. You hand over to me anything you have that could make trouble for Kaye's brother. In return I'll stay quiet about what I know about Ainsworth Securities, and with any luck you'll stay out of jail.''

"You're bluffing!" Vane sneered, but he'd gone a little pale.

"I'm not," Jack said simply. "I've got documents that show how you manipulated the share price prior to the takeover. The fraud squad would just love to get their hands on them. But if you think I'm bluffing, go ahead."

There was a silence.

"Harry here will accompany you to your office and collect anything that incriminates Paul," Jack continued. "I want it all. Don't try keeping anything back."

Vane breathed hard. "In return I want whatever you've got."

"You won't get it," Jack said. "Quit bothering me. You haven't any cards to play."

Vane's lips tightened into a hard line, making him harsh and terrible. But Jack, meeting his gaze, wore a similar look. For a moment Kaye caught a glimpse of something formidable, even ruthless, beneath Jack's smiling good nature. Vane's eyes fell first.

"Be damned to you!" he said viciously.

"Take these with you," Kaye said, stripping off her diamonds. "I want nothing you've ever given me."

He snatched them from her angrily, then turned on Rhoda. "And you!" he raged. "You get nothing for nothing."

He reached out and wrenched the brooch off her shoulder. Rhoda screamed and burst into tears of rage. Vane seemed about to speak, but something in Jack's face made him think better of it. He turned and stalked out, followed by Harry.

Sam and Bertie let out a roar of delight. Rhoda's lips were tight with fury. Paul looked uneasy. Kaye could hardly take in what had happened. Then she realized the nightmare was over. She was free of Lewis Vane. She gave a gasp and covered her mouth with her hands.

"Hey, there," Jack said, taking her by the shoulders. "It's finished. Everything's all right."

"I can't believe it," she choked. "Is it really happening?"

"It's happening," he assured her. "You won't see him again."

"But how did you do it? All those things you said about Ainsworth Securities—?"

"It's no secret that he pulled a fast one over that deal, although nobody's been able to pin it on him."

"But—you said you had documents..."

Jack grinned, showing strong, white teeth. It was the grin of a pirate, ribald, knowing, wickedly mischievous, and it lit up the world.

"You mean it wasn't true?" Kaye breathed.

"'Course it wasn't true," Sam said triumphantly. "Half of what he says isn't true." He slapped his son on the back. "I taught this boy everything he knows," he said proudly.

"You were bluffing the whole time?" Kaye said, awed.

Jack took her hands in his. "Kaye, darling—" the word slipped out of its own accord "—that's how it's done. Bluff and counterbluff. I've bluffed millions when my pockets were empty."

"But suppose Lewis had called your bluff?"

"He wouldn't dare. And even if he did, you aren't marrying him. If there's a court case I'll get Paul the best lawyer there is. He'll get probation or a suspended sentence."

She tightened her hands on his and he caught his breath at the beautiful fervor in her eyes. "Paul *will* be all right, won't he?"

His brow creased. "Don't you ever think of anyone but Paul?"

"I was only marrying Lewis for his sake. Thank you so much for saving him."

"I wasn't saving him," Jack said quizzically. "I was saving you."

"Him—me—what difference does it make? Thank you anyway."

Rhoda was nearly dancing with rage. "Look at me," she fulminated, pointing to the tear in her jacket where the brooch had been. "*Look what he did to me!*" She burst into angry tears.

Despite everything, Kaye was torn by the sound of her mother's weeping. She tried to put her arms about Rhoda.

"Don't cry, Mom," she begged.

Rhoda threw her off. "It's all your fault," she said hysterically. "I hope you're pleased with yourself. You've thrown away the chance of a lifetime—"

"But Paul's going to be all right," Kaye protested.

"And what about the help Lewis could have given him in future? With Lewis behind him, Paul had it made."

"I doubt it," Jack told her. "Once Vane got what he wanted he wouldn't have bothered with Paul again, except as a weapon against Kaye. You must be very relieved that your daughter has escaped that fate.''

Rhoda scowled at him, but Paul, more sharp-witted than his mother, was beginning to see where his own best interests lay. "I'm glad you're not going to marry him, sis, honestly," he said warmly. "It doesn't matter about me, as long as you don't suffer."

"Easy to say that now the danger's past," Bertie growled just loud enough for Jack to hear.

"I agree," he replied quietly. "Why doesn't she tell those two where to get off?"

"She's never been able to fight them," Bertie said, holding out his glass for Sam to refill. "Kaye's too softhearted for her own good. They're her mother and brother, and she wants to believe the best of them, despite the way they act. I've tried to stand up for her, but I've never done much good."

"You did one thing," Jack said, meeting his eyes. And a significant look passed between them.

Kaye was hugging Paul, passionately grateful for his words. "Thank you, darling," she said. "I knew you'd understand."

"Well, I don't!" Rhoda snapped. "I'll never forgive you for this, my girl. Never. I suppose you're going to move in here as his fancy woman. *You'll* be all right, won't you? Never mind anyone else. But you'll get your comeuppance. When he's had enough he'll chuck you out on your ear, and it'll serve you right. Don't come to me for sympathy."

"I'm sure she wouldn't dream of it," Jack said dryly. "And your daughter—" he emphasized the words very slightly "—won't be my 'fancy woman.' I want her to come and care for Georgy."

"You made her give up a rich husband to be a flaming nursemaid?" Rhoda almost shrieked.

Then Jack said, "She's not going to be a nursemaid. She's going to be my wife."

Total stunned silence.

Everyone stared at him. Even Jack was inwardly staring at himself, wondering where the words had come from. Whatever he'd meant to say, it wasn't that.

"Jack," Kaye breathed as if she couldn't believe her ears, "you can't mean…"

"'Course he doesn't mean it," Rhoda scoffed. "He's stringing you along."

"Don't talk to my future wife like that," Jack said, his eyes kindling.

"But Mom's right," Kaye stammered. "You don't need to— I mean, you can't want to marry me."

"I *need* to marry you," he said, taking her hands. "When Elsie turns up here demanding Georgy, I have to be able to show that I've got a stable home. You promised, Kaye."

She longed to say yes, but it was too much like a dream come true. She would gladly make sacrifices for Jack, but she didn't want him to make any.

"I'll stay here, anyway," she said. "I'll keep my promise."

"To do that you have to marry me," he said firmly. "I need a wife to show Elsie, a mother for Georgy."

"Now you're talking," Rhoda said.

"Mom, please," Kaye said desperately. She was torn, longing to say yes, but fearful of snatching a prize that seemed too good for her.

"Don't be a fool," Rhoda sneered. "If he's willing to do the right thing by you, grab him."

"I'm not going to 'grab' him," Kaye cried.

"Of course not," Paul said quickly. "Kaye isn't like that." He slipped an arm around her shoulders. "Don't do anything you don't want to, sis."

Bertie snorted loudly.

Kaye put her hands to her face to cover her burning cheeks. "If only I knew what to do," she whispered.

"You do what's best for you," Paul urged. He looked around at his luxurious surroundings. "Mind you, it mightn't be so bad. And of course, if you owe this guy like he says... But it's your choice."

"I do owe him," Kaye said. "Jack, if this is really what you want..."

"It's what I want," Jack confirmed.

"Then I'll marry you."

Bertie and Sam cheered and finished the bottle. Jack smiled into Kaye's eyes, making her heart turn over wildly. She didn't understand why she'd agreed, but then she didn't understand anything that was happening. She'd started today as the bride of a man she hated, and now she was going to marry the man she'd carried in her heart for years. It was too much, too quickly.

Paul was full of glee, whirling Kaye around and around and hugging her tightly. Kaye hugged him back, thrilled that he was safe. Jack watched them with a little frown.

Rhoda sniffed, torn between satisfaction at getting a rich man into the family after all, anger at the way her despised daughter had fallen on her feet, and outrage at the way Jack had spoken to her.

"Just you make sure he sticks to it," she said spitefully. "There's many a slip twixt cup and lip."

"There'll be no slips," Jack said evenly, only his good manners concealing his dislike. "We'll marry as soon as possible."

He turned away. He needed a moment to come to terms with his own rash action. He'd had no thought of marriage, but when he'd seen Kaye's family bullying her he'd been overwhelmed by the desire to defend her against them, and had said the first thing that came into his head. He was a warmhearted, impulsive man, and it had led him into many rash decisions in the past. But this was the rashest, and now he was wondering exactly what he'd done.

Then the gambler's instinct that had carried him through so many glorious risks in the past rose up in him again. He'd thrown the dice and seen how they fell, and he would carry it through to the end.

"I think that settles everything," he said. "The wedding will be in three days."

"You can't fix up a wedding in that time," Rhoda insisted.

"I can," he said simply. "I'll get a special license. Kaye will call you tomorrow with the full details. Kaye, I hope you don't mind staying here in the meantime. We have a lot of arrangements to make."

"Oh, yes." Rhoda sniffed. "We all know where that will end."

"I beg your pardon," Jack said, a warning note in his voice.

Rhoda failed to heed it. "Lock your bedroom door, my girl, or your second wedding will get canceled as fast your first."

"Please don't speak like that in front of my daughter,'' Jack said coldly. ''Otherwise I'll have to ask you to leave.''

Rhoda went scarlet with anger, but before she could speak Sam intervened, at his most mischievous. ''Don't you worry about Kaye, ma'am. My pal Bertie is staying here to protect her virtue.''

They all turned to look at Bertie, who was leaning back on the sofa, happily tipsy, totally useless.

''Don't be ridiculous,'' Rhoda said through gritted teeth.

''Honestly,'' Sam persisted. ''He'll stand outside her bedroom door all night with a big stick, and if my son tries to have his evil way, Bertie will bop him one.''

''*Sam,* will you grow up?'' Jack demanded, sounding harassed. ''Bertie, I'll be glad to have you stay. It will make Kaye happier, but I promise you, there'll be no need for sentry duty. And you,'' he added, turning to his daughter, ''can wipe that grin off your face.''

''Yes, Dad,'' she said woodenly.

''Kaye, why don't you say goodbye to your folks now? Then Mary can show you upstairs.''

Kaye embraced her mother, receiving the smallest possible response. Paul hugged her and kept his arm around her waist until they reached the foot of the stairs. Paul's prospects were improving by the moment.

In a daze Kaye climbed the wide stairs and went along the corridor until Mary flung open the door of a bedroom.

''We weren't sure how things would work out,'' she said, ''so Jack said to have a room ready for you, just in case. I hope you like it.''

It was a large room, with floor-length windows at one end leading to a small balcony. Despite its luxury it had a homely feel.

"You've got a little bathroom through here," Mary said, showing her. "And how would you like a cup of tea?"

"I could murder for a cup of tea," Kaye said thankfully.

As Mary left the room Georgy came in, bearing a pile of clothes. "I've brought you some of my own gear," she said. "We're about the same size now."

Kaye glanced through the pile with misgiving, trying to picture herself in clothes designed for a girl of fourteen. But Georgy's taste was unexpectedly good, and she found some stylish green suede pants and a fawn shirt that went well with them. As the girl had said, they were the same size, except that Georgy's figure was the more voluptuous of the two.

She helped Kaye strip off the white satin. "We'll need to get you another wedding dress," she said, considering. "In fact, we'll have to go out this afternoon."

"Georgy—" Kaye protested.

"We've got to buy things fast, if Dad's planning a wedding in three days. That's so like him. He makes up his mind and *zoom!* It has to be now, *now!*"

"Yes, I'm beginning to understand that," Kaye said worriedly. "Doesn't he ever regret these impulsive decisions?"

"If he does, he doesn't let on," Georgy said. "He says his instincts never let him down."

"But my family pushed him into this. They didn't give him any choice."

Georgy hooted with disrespectful laughter. *"Dad?"* she shrieked. "He never does anything he doesn't want to. If people try to push him he just gets more stubborn."

"Really?" Kaye said hopefully.

"I promise you, Dad wasn't pushed," Georgy said. Her voice was kind, making her look and sound oddly mature.

"Tea up!" Mary called, reappearing with a tray.

There were sandwiches and biscuits as well, reminding Kaye that she'd eaten nothing since she got up that morning. Suddenly she was ravenous. The nightmare had lifted and the world was full of hope again.

Chapter Three

There was a knock on the door. "Can I come in?" Jack called.

"It's okay, she's decent," Georgy called back.

Jack nodded his appreciation when he saw Kaye. "They've all gone," he said, "so we can start making plans. Sorry to simply take you over like that, but it wouldn't have been a good idea for you to go home with your mother."

"No," Kaye agreed, shuddering at the thought.

"But Kaye doesn't have any clothes," Georgy said, "so I think we should get her some this afternoon."

"Good thinking." Jack pointed to the discarded wedding dress. "Was that bought or hired?"

"Bought," Kaye told him. "Lewis insisted on it, and kept telling me how much he'd spent."

"Fine. Mary, please return it to Lewis Vane."

Georgy giggled. "What will he do with a wedding dress?"

"I don't know, but it belongs to him," Jack said. "I'm leaving him no excuse to make trouble."

"Lewis doesn't like to let anything go to waste," Kaye observed. "He'll probably save it for his next bride." She shuddered, and gasped, "Oh, I'm so glad to be free of him."

She sat down suddenly, shaking, and hid her face in her hands. Georgy and Mary made instinctive movements toward her, but Jack discouraged them both with a look. A slight gesture in the direction of the door sent them out.

He sat down beside Kaye and put both arms around her in a bear hug that was immensely comforting. "Hey, there," he said. "No need to get upset."

"But only this morning when I got up—I thought—"

"You thought you were going to marry Prince Charming, and now you're stuck with me instead," he teased.

She gave a little choke of laughter. "If you knew how I dreaded the thought of marrying him—and now… I can't believe the nightmare may be over."

"What's this 'may be'? Vane won't bother you again, I promise."

"But is Paul safe, really safe? Jack, you don't know how spiteful Lewis can be when he's thwarted."

"I've said I'll take care of him for you."

"And for Paul?"

"Yes, for Paul, if that's what it takes to make you happy."

"You must think I'm crazy. I know Paul is a bit

immature, but it's not all his fault. Mom's spoiled him."

"Is she the only one?" he asked gently. "How come he thinks he can hide behind your skirts?"

"Because I've always let him," she admitted. "Maybe I shouldn't have, but I've looked after him all my life. He was such a lovely little boy—"

"And now he's a grown man who should be standing on his own feet," Jack said firmly. "The best thing that could happen to him would be a spell in jail."

"Oh, no—you promised. Jack, you promised!"

For a moment her face was wild with fear and he stared at her, shocked. "It's all right," he said at last. "I gave you my word and I'll keep it. Kaye, I won't let him go to jail. Trust me."

"Of course I do," she said shakily.

The sound of the car returning prevented further talk. He hurried down to meet Harry in the hall. Without a word Harry handed his boss a brown envelope, and Jack went through the contents quickly.

"Fine," he said at last. "Did he give you any trouble?"

"He tried arguing a bit," the giant said. "I just stood and looked through him until he gave up wasting energy."

"Go and have something to eat. It's going to be a busy afternoon."

He returned to Kaye and in silence handed her the evidence that incriminated Paul, watching her whole body relax as she studied it. At last she looked up, and Jack caught his breath at the blinding joy he saw in her face.

"You did it," she breathed. "You really did it!"

"I told you I would."

"It's finished," she said in a disbelieving voice. "Oh, Jack, thank you so much."

"Don't I get a kiss as a reward?" he asked, grinning.

It had been half a joke, but the next moment she tossed the papers onto the bed and threw herself into his arms in a passion of emotion.

He embraced her in return, enjoying the feel of her eager body pressed against his. He'd held her once before, on the island, when they'd so nearly made love. Nobody would ever know what it had cost him to call a halt. She'd been melting and lovely, and he'd ached to feel her beneath him, welcoming him into her.

It had taken all his self-control to push her away and try to speak in a normal voice. Her grief had touched his heart and he'd almost weakened, but stronger than desire had been tenderness, and the need to protect her.

Now she was in his arms again, reminding him of all he'd given up with regret, promising everything for the future. Her face was raised to his, happy, inviting, and he smiled as he laid his mouth over hers. He'd meant it lightly, but she felt so good that he stayed as he was, enjoying the sensation, tempted to explore further but knowing that this was the wrong time.

His problem was solved for him by the sound of the door opening, and Georgy's voice saying, "Whoops, sorry!"

"Come in," Jack said in a resigned voice, releasing Kaye. He smiled into her eyes, which were bright and ardent. "Soon," he whispered, and she nodded eagerly.

"Dad, I don't think you ought to do that," Georgy said in a shocked voice. "After your promise—"

"Cut it out, young lady," he warned her, and Georgy giggled.

The promise had been half a joke, but it alarmed him slightly to realize that it could go hang. If his daughter hadn't burst in he might have yielded to temptation. He was a man who lived an intensely physical life, his sensations always close to the surface. Those few brief moments of holding Kaye against him had aroused not only his desire but also his curiosity. He remembered the night of their "almost loving" clearly enough to be tantalized by his unexpected bride.

Her build was still delicate, but she'd filled out a little since then, become a woman. The lush wedding dress had concealed the details, and in any case, he'd been watching her face, with its fascinating mixture of youth and sadness. But now she was nearly his, and he was intrigued to know if he was going to regret his rash action. Watching her peachy complexion and the sparkling light in her gray eyes, he rather thought he wasn't.

"Still sure you want to be her stepmother?" he asked, trying to speak normally.

"I'll take my chances," Kaye said, and his sharp ears detected that she, too, was a little breathless.

"You'd better go and get kitted out. I'll have to entrust you to Georgy's tender mercies, as I can't spare Mary."

"I've got some clothes at home," Kaye said, uneasy at throwing herself entirely on Jack's charity. "I mean, things I paid for myself."

"I appreciate that, but I don't want you to go back there. Better for us to start from scratch."

"We're going to have a great time," Georgy said, thrilled at the prospect of a shopping trip. "You'll need things to wear on your honeymoon—"

"I'm afraid that'll have to come later," Jack interrupted. "I've got the boat trial in a few days, and I can't put it off, because my option's running out."

"Dad crashed a speedboat last month," Georgy explained. "He got pretty smashed up, so of course he can't wait to try it again."

"Yes, I saw it in the paper," Kaye said, recalling. "You're going back so soon? Isn't it dangerous?"

"Of course it's dangerous," Jack said, baffled.

"It's no fun otherwise," Georgy translated. "It'll be terribly exciting. Dad always drives to the limit."

"Go and call a cab, Georgy," Jack said. "I can't even spare Harry this afternoon."

The room was quieter when Georgy had vanished. Jack smiled awkwardly. "You'll get used to her. Sorry about the honeymoon."

"I hadn't even thought about it," she assured him. "There's too much to take in at once as it is."

"Yes, let's go one step at a time," he said with a touch of relief. "I'll leave you to get ready."

"Won't all the shops will be closed by now?"

"It's only one o'clock."

"Oh, yes, of course." Kaye rubbed her eyes. "So much has happened already today that I've lost my bearings."

"Me, too. I spent last night on a plane, and went

straight to the church from the airport. My head's still in New York and my stomach's lost all track of time. But the day's still young, and we must make the most of it.''

It was Kaye's second experience of buying clothes at her groom's expense, but it was a world away from the first. For one thing, there was Georgy, who was her mother's daughter when it came to a really imaginative spending spree. Despite her youth she had a shrewd sense of style.

She concentrated on Dorrell's, a huge store in London's luxurious Mayfair area, where Jack had an account. The staff knew her and fell over themselves to serve her. When they learned that Kaye was the future Mrs. Masefield they treated her with new respect. Jack's name was barely mentioned, but she felt she was learning more about him by the minute.

Dresses, shoes, coats, underwear: the pile grew as Georgy signed papers with gay abandon. At first Kaye demurred, but her protests grew fainter as she saw that the girl was also seizing the chance to augment her own wardrobe. Besides, she herself looked like a dream in her new clothes. And that was how she wanted to look, for Jack.

They finished up in the store restaurant, in a state of near collapse. ''You look as if you need refueling,'' Georgy remarked kindly.

''I do. I'm dead on my feet,'' Kaye admitted.

Georgy ordered them a hearty meal, and while they were eating it she began to ask Kaye about herself. ''I know we met before,'' she said, ''but that was six years ago. It's like starting again. Just think of your being ready to marry that creep, just for Paul. You must be awfully fond of him.''

''Yes, very.''

''Is he as nice as he looks?''

Kaye realized that Georgy really wanted to talk about Paul, so she obliged her with stories from their childhood, choosing those that showed her brother in the best light.

After a while the conversation turned to their purchases.

''What do you think of that green dress I bought?'' Georgy wanted to know.

''Far too old for you. Your father will say the same.''

The girl gave a shrug of her slim, elegant shoulders and pronounced airily, ''Dad's going gaga in his old age.''

''Old age?'' Kaye echoed. ''Oh, right. He must be all of thirty-seven.''

''Well, not until his next birthday, actually,'' Georgy conceded large-mindedly. ''But this step-mother business, 'keep Georgy in order,' that sort of thing. It's a laugh. Look, I'm happy for him to marry you. I think you're a really nice person. But I live my own life. Okay?''

''You seem to have it all sussed out,'' Kaye said mildly.

''I have. I'm not a kid anymore, but he won't see that. I mean, dragging me back here the way he did. Henri didn't like it.''

''Henri?''

''My boyfriend. He's dreamy.''

''I thought Paul had caught your eye.''

"Oh, sure, but a woman really needs more than one string to her bow, don't you think?" Georgy asked with a world-weary air.

Kaye smiled. "How would your father feel if I took that literally?"

"Oh, not you, of course. You've made a commitment to Dad, but I'm still playing the field. Henri's missing me wildly, passionately, desperately."

"He's been in touch?"

"I called him."

"Georgy, you shouldn't have done that," Kaye said instinctively.

The girl bristled. "I do as I like."

"Of course, but it wasn't 'cool,'" Kaye said, hastily recovering lost ground. "You should have waited for him to call you." Kaye was improvising madly, for cunning behavior was foreign to her, but it was vital for Georgy to feel she was on her side. "Never look eager."

Georgy considered. "I guess you're right. Hey, you're not bad for an 'old.' Anyway, I expect Henri will be here soon to take me away. That's why it's so disgusting of Dad to make me go back to school. Would you believe, I have to wear a *uniform?* I'll just die if Henri finds me looking like a schoolgirl."

"What do you mean, 'back to school'? Didn't you go to school before?"

"Are you kidding? School's for wimps."

Kaye began to understand why Jack needed her so badly.

They arrived home to find a mountain of deliveries already there. Mary greeted them with the news that the special license was sorted out, and the wedding was set.

"Of course," Georgy said gleefully. "Things always happen the way Dad wants them to. Where is he?"

"He's had to go out, but Sam's in. I'm off home now. See you in the morning."

"But tomorrow's Sunday," Kaye objected. "Don't tell me he keeps you working on Sunday, too."

"Not usually. But preparing a wedding and a reception for three hundred people is quite a task."

"Three hundred people." Kaye gulped. "I thought it was going to be a quiet affair."

"That *is* quiet, for Jack. Bye."

Kaye had no time to recover from this speech before Bertie and Sam descended on them, sweeping them off to supper and demanding to know all about their purchases. The two old men were as instantly at home with each other as they'd been six years ago. They back chatted constantly, finishing each other's sentences and happily swapping rude names.

Kaye let it all flow over her, feeling sleepily content. But she wished Jack would come home, so that she could believe this was real.

When supper was over she slipped outside, needing to be alone. Jack's garden was huge and gave her plenty of space to lose herself in the gathering dusk. She wandered along the paths between the well-tended lawns and trees, feeling the cool evening air on her cheeks, wondering if she would awaken in a moment to find it had all been a beautiful dream, and she must marry Lewis Vane after all.

"Kaye! Are you there? Kaye?"

She turned, eager at the sound of Jack's voice. He was no dream, but a solidly real man, who was already taking hold of her heart as firmly as he'd done long ago. "I'm here," she called.

Darkness was falling fast and it was a moment before he could discern her, sitting on a bench that ran right around a huge oak tree. "Did you come out here to escape the riot?" he asked, grinning.

"Well, it really is nice and quiet."

"Sorry to leave you to Georgy's tender mercies, but I had to fix some details about the boat trial. You've no idea what you've let yourself in for."

"It can't be worse than what I've escaped," she said lightly.

"That's true," he said with a grin. "Whenever I become unbearable, just remind yourself of Lewis Vane."

"Jack," she said suddenly, "are you really sure about this?"

"Too late now. I've booked the church and twisted arms to get the license. You can't cancel two weddings to two different men in one week. People will think you're strange or something."

It was no good going on. She was helpless against his determination to pass it off as a joke. It was a reminder of something he'd hinted about on Singleton. Jack's easy good nature was delightful, but he could use it as a defense mechanism.

"I've seen the piles of boxes from this afternoon," he said, skillfully putting her question behind them, still unanswered.

"They're not all mine," Kaye said anxiously. "Georgy did some shopping, too."

"If I know Georgy, she did most of the shopping."

"She was telling me about Henri, her boyfriend."

"Not while I have breath in my body," Jack said grimly. "He's the younger brother of François, Elsie's latest toyboy. Elsie has a villa in Monte Carlo, and when François moved in with her, so did Henri, looking for pickings."

"What about Valerie, the nanny?"

"She left last year. Elsie didn't replace her. But Val would have known how to deal with Henri. He's good-looking in a greasy way, and he was making eyes at Georgy when I turned up. Elsie wasn't even there. She and François had gone off to the casino, leaving Georgy alone in the house with Henri. I told her to pack her bags."

"And she came with you willingly?"

"More or less. She'd just had a dustup with Elsie, and I suppose she thought she'd play us off against each other. She wasn't so pleased when she found living with me meant attending school and going to bed early."

"What happened when Elsie came back and found her gone?"

"I left her a letter, saying Georgy was safe. Elsie got on the phone to me and screamed blue murder."

"But didn't she follow you here?"

"No," Jack said, his eyes kindling with anger. "Because of François. He's a lot younger than her, and very much in demand. Elsie keeps hold of him with gifts and money, but she daren't take her eyes off him. So far she hasn't shown up, but her lawyer is bombarding me with demands for Georgy's return."

"But how could any court order you to give her

up?'' Kaye wondered. ''Once you tell them how things were—''

''It's not easy to convince a court that a girl doesn't belong with her mother, especially when she's always lived with her. And they've got a firm of private investigators trying to dig up some dirt on me.''

''Can they?''

Jack's vivid grin had a touch of wryness. ''I've enjoyed my life to the full. There are a few things that might make me seem a dubious moral authority for a young girl. I need to show that all that stuff is behind me.''

''And our marriage will do that,'' she agreed. There was a deep pleasure in the thought that she was giving him back something in return for all he'd given her. And her heart yearned toward him. He might not love her, but he needed her, and by living close to him she would have the chance to win his love.

He leaned back against the tree, yawning, and she recalled what he'd said earlier. ''Did you really spend last night on a plane?'' she asked.

''It was the only way to get here in time. As it was, there was a delay, and I only made it by the skin of my teeth.''

''I couldn't believe it was really you standing there, after all these years, coming to my rescue like a knight in shining armor.''

''I'm no knight in armor,'' Jack said with a plain man's discomfort at ''fancy talk.''

''All right, the cavalry galloping to the rescue, then.''

''That's better. Besides, it's you that's galloped to my rescue. You'll find Georgy a handful.''

"But she's charming. We got on wonderfully well this afternoon."

"She was getting you onto her side," Jack said darkly. "With Georgy, charm and manipulation go hand in hand. She gets it from her mother."

"From her mother?" Kaye echoed. "Oh, really?"

She let the implication hang in the air, and after a moment Jack laughed ruefully. "Well, maybe not only from Elsie. Poor Georgy! What a legacy for a kid! Elsie on the one hand and me on the other. But with your help, it's not too late to save her." He laid his hand on hers. "What shall I get you for a wedding present?"

"You've already given me the thing I wanted most."

Paul's safety, he thought, and knew an unexpected pang. He was used to women who were chiefly attracted by his money, but never before one who saw him as a good-luck charm for her brother. It was a novel experience, and he would try to deal with it without rancor.

"You don't mind too much marrying me, do you?" he asked.

He thought he saw a strange look flicker across her face, but the light was too dim to be sure. It was a moment before she spoke, and then only to say, "I owe you."

"Kaye," he protested, "I wouldn't claim a promise like that if it was against your will. What do you think I am? Another Lewis Vane?"

"It's not against my will," she promised.

"Paul's safe now. You don't have to go through with it if you'd rather not."

"Hey, what is this?" she asked. "Are you trying to get out of marrying me?"

"Giving you the chance to get out—if that's what you want."

Again he had the sensation that she was thinking something she couldn't tell him. But then he met her eyes and found something in them that made him forget speech. He slipped his arms about her, murmuring, "Don't we have some unfinished business from this afternoon?"

"I believe you're right," she said.

He kissed her tentatively, asking questions but not waiting for the answers. Beneath his unruffled air he was as shaken as Kaye by the speed of events. This morning she'd been almost a stranger, the excuse for one of those adventures that were the breath of life to him. Tonight she was his promised wife. His head was spinning. Or perhaps that was her effect.

"Do you know," he murmured, "I'm breaking every promise I made to your family."

"No, you're not," she whispered back. "You said you wouldn't come knocking on my bedroom door. You didn't say anything about the garden."

He laughed against her mouth. "My thoughts are a violation of every promise I made."

"So who's checking?"

The boldness of her teasing reply caught him off guard. Decidedly she was full of surprises. It was hard to believe that this was the same Kaye he'd seen only that morning, nervous and intimidated by her family. That young woman had aroused Jack's protectiveness. The one in his arms aroused very different feelings. She was bewitching in her innocent sensuality, and he was swept by a fierce urge to carry her to bed there and then.

It was a novel experience for him to have to restrain his impulses. But he contented himself with moving his hands over her slim contours, noting curves and hollows and promising himself a more thorough investigation some time in the not too distant future.

"Kaye? Hallo? Is anybody there?"

Bertie's voice broke rudely in on them, forcing Jack to release her. "Bertie's taking his chaperon duties a sight too seriously for my liking." He sighed. "Never mind. Our moment will come."

"Yes," she whispered. "Oh, Jack—yes...."

She rose quickly and ran to meet Bertie. Together they walked back to the house, leaving Jack sitting under the tree, very thoughtful.

Sam found him still there an hour later. "Not like you to spend a lot of time brooding, son," he remarked, sitting beside him.

"I've got a lot to brood about, haven't I?"

"I'll say! When we set this up, you never said you were planning to marry her."

"I wasn't planning it. It happened on the spur of the moment. Suddenly it just—felt right."

"That was this morning," Sam observed shrewdly. "Does it still feel right?"

"It feels more right with every moment that passes, and I don't know why. I could give you reasons. She's delightful and charming, but so are others that I never thought of marrying."

"Been carrying a torch for six years?"

"Me? You know me better than that. I'm not the

sentimental kind. I can't explain the way I feel, but it's right, I do know that.''

"Coming inside?"

"No, I think I'll stay out here for a while. I've still got some thinking to do."

Sam paused as he walked away, and looked back, hesitating. ''Maybe it's going to be all right for you, after all,'' he said.

"What do you mean by that?"

"You know what I mean, son, as well as I do."

Jack stayed alone in the dark. Sam's lighthearted remark had confronted him with something he'd only half realized before. For six years he'd remembered Kaye when he'd forgotten others, because there was something special about her, something— He hated analyzing things, and finally gave it up. Just "something special." She was lovely in an understated way, but it wasn't physical. It was to do with the light that radiated from her.

He remembered the first night on Singleton, how she'd insisted on telling him that they weren't as rich as they seemed. *We're frauds,* she'd said, as though that was the worst thing in the world. That had been his first brush with the honesty that ruled her character.

He lived in a world of fraud, most of which wore a pleasant face. He was used to women who wanted something from him and were prepared to use their bodies to get it. His relationships with them were a series of bargains, good-natured and openhanded on his part, but never going deeper than a certain level. He'd never thought of marrying any of them.

But Kaye was special. He'd recognized as much even then. She was as enduring as the earth, as fresh and true as sparkling water. She was real. And he'd known it when he'd backed her into a corner and virtually forced her to marry him.

But she, too, had made a bargain. She was marrying him in part to redeem her promise, but also to help her weakling brother, and perhaps to hide from her dreadful mother. Fair enough, in return for what she was giving him.

As for love, he remembered the soft bloom of her skin, the feel of her slim body against his, her arms about his neck, giving passion with a full heart, as she did everything. He imagined the night, soon to come, when she would be completely his.

When he thought of that, and felt his own body's ungovernable response, he felt that love might safely be left to take care of itself.

He was humming as he returned to the house.

Chapter Four

Kaye's second wedding in three days was a world away from her first. Her dress was long, and made of snow white silk, but cut on restrained lines and unadorned. The veil, too, was simple, held in place by a delicate pearl tiara, a gift from Jack.

Sam was the best man, and Georgy insisted on being bridesmaid because, as she said with charming frankness, it meant a lovely new dress. She found a soft peach silk that suited her perfectly. As before, Bertie escorted the bride to church to give her away.

This time she was happy to go to her wedding. The sight of her groom turning to watch her coming down the aisle filled her with delight, and she walked the last few yards with a smile on her face. Jack's own smile answered her, and his clasp on her hand was warm and reassuring.

He even had a joke to share with her. When the vicar reached the words about ''just cause and impediment,'' Jack gave a quick glance over his shoulder, as if to remind her what had happened last time. The inquiring lift of his eyebrows was wicked, and they met each other's eyes for a long moment, until the vicar coughed.

After that the marriage service proceeded without incident. Kaye happily made the vows she'd dreaded making only a few days ago. Jack spoke his promises in a steady, confident voice, and slipped the ring onto her finger. At last it was over, and the organ pealed out as they turned to go back down the aisle.

At once Kaye felt Jack stiffen.

At the entrance to the church stood a woman, arms akimbo, watching them with a cynical look on her face.

''Oh, no!'' Jack muttered under his breath. ''Elsie!''

Everything seemed to stop while Jack regarded the distant figure of his ex-wife with horror. ''Elsie,'' he said again. ''How did she manage to get here?''

Kaye squeezed his hand. ''It doesn't matter. You've got me now.''

He squeezed back. ''Thank goodness for that! Right, here we go!''

As they moved slowly toward the woman, Kaye got a better look at her. She knew from Sam that Elsie was forty-five, but she was well preserved, with a lean body and a face that had received much care and attention. She might have been attractive but for the jeering expression she wore as she watched the bride and groom. Kaye flinched under that look, then put her head up, refusing to be cowed. This woman was

the enemy against whom Jack had begged her help.
And she wouldn't let him down.

For a moment when it seemed as if Elsie might
actually bar their way out of the church, but at the last
moment she stood aside with a scornful curl of the lip.
Then they were out in the bright sun, with a little
breeze whirling Kaye's veil up into the air.

Sam had seen the danger, and acted fast, descending
on Elsie with an air of joviality, but actually taking
her firmly in charge.

"Hallo, Sam." She greeted him with a scornful
smile.

He wasted no time on politeness. "I don't know
what you hope to gain by this, but if you try to spoil
their day I'll wring your neck like the scrawny chicken
you're fast becoming."

The smirk vanished. "Why, you—"

"Shut up and don't move until the photos are finished."

The pictures took a while—the whole party, with
Rhoda done up to the nines and Paul looking boyishly
pretty, then various combinations, the bride and groom
with Sam and Bertie, with Georgy in front, the bride
and groom with Georgy, and finally just the two of
them. Jack drew her close, kissing her perfectly for the
camera, and Kaye had a twinge of happy anticipation.
Everything in her responded to his kiss, reminding her
of the night to come, when she would find the fulfillment that had been deferred for six years. She loved
him with all her heart, and she wanted him urgently.

Sam and Bertie escorted Elsie to the reception, with
her sitting between them in the car—like a prisoner as
she afterward complained. Once there, Sam thrust a

glass of champagne in her hand and threatened her with dire retribution if she opened her mouth too soon.

"We'll just have to try and keep her quiet until the guests have gone," he muttered to Bertie.

Jack was a well-known, colorful figure, marrying with exactly the kind of unpredictable drama that people would have expected of him, and nobody wanted to miss the show. So, despite the short notice, the guests numbered nearly three hundred. They spilled out onto the lawn where the tables were laid in the open. Overhead was a hastily erected lattice roof, hung with festoons of flowers. More flowers adorned the tables, and the long table at the top, to which Jack led his bride, was adorned with a profusion of white roses.

The crowd was large enough to neutralize Elsie for a while. Recognizing a temporary setback, she drained her champagne before launching herself dramatically onto her daughter. "Georgy, *darling,* did you think Mommy wasn't coming for you?"

"Hi, Mom," Georgy said cheerfully.

"Let me look at you, baby. Let me see my little Georgy." She held her by the shoulders, at arm's length, and surveyed Georgy's peach dress. "No, I don't think that color's quite you."

The girl's smile faded. "I think it is."

"It's just a teeny bit washed out for you." Elsie's superficial mind was momentarily absorbed in this detail.

"Mom, this is Paul," Georgy said brightly. "Paul, this is my mom."

Nobody would have called Paul a mighty intelligence, but he had a shrewd instinct for what his charm could and couldn't achieve. Now that instinct told him to lay it on with a trowel. He clasped Elsie's hand in a warm grip, and smiled into her eyes.

"I've really looked forward to meeting you, ma'am," he said with just the right touch of sincerity. "Georgy's told me so much about you. I hope it's all true. But I think there's been some mistake? You can't be her mother. More like her older sister."

"Young man, that one had whiskers on it when I was in my cradle," Elsie told him severely. But her eyes gleamed with appreciation of his youthful, well-made figure.

Guests were milling about the tables, searching for their place names. There was none for Elsie, but she solved that problem by parking herself firmly in the seat she wanted, ignoring the feeble protests of its rightful owner. She now had a perfect view of the bride and groom.

"Ignore her," Jack whispered. "She can't trouble us." He carried her hand to his lips, and the guests cheered.

Mary was clearly an organizing genius. In three days she'd masterminded the bridal feast, the flowers, the music. Only the weather was beyond her control, but here the luck was with her, and although summer hadn't really started, the sun shone warmly.

Kaye guessed that they were all wondering why Jack had married such an ordinary little brown mouse, on the spur of the moment. She was too shy to feel comfortable about this, but she kept her head high, and smiled. Jack seemed to understand, for now and then his huge warm hand would engulf her slender one, and a smile of reassurance was in his eyes. Gradually she relaxed. With Jack's support she could manage anything. If only this was over, she thought, and she could be alone with him to enjoy her happiness to the full.

Together they cut the cake, and then the band struck up. A temporary dance floor had been set up on the lawn, and Jack and Kaye had the first dance, to loud applause. Afterward they began to circulate among the guests, and soon Kaye found herself standing face-to-face with Jack's first wife. Elsie had drunk just enough champagne to make her belligerent, and she looked her ex-husband's bride up and down in a cynical, appraising way. Kaye met her gaze steadily, refusing to be intimidated, and taking the chance to size Elsie up in her turn.

She saw a woman with cold eyes and a face marked by discontent and self-indulgence. It was Sam who'd told her the details of how Elsie had gotten Jack in her sights when he was twenty-one and she was eight years older. Even at that age he'd already been on his way to a fortune, old in the ways of finance, but still green in the ways of women. Elsie had fascinated him, and when she contrived to become pregnant, he'd married her.

"She didn't care tuppence for Jack, or the kiddy," Sam had confided. "But Georgy gave her a hold over him, so when she left him for another man the poor little mite got dragged from pillar to post. Elsie's had a good few affairs since then. In the beginning the men left her richer. Now her looks are going and they leech off her. Don't believe her devoted-mother act. Georgy's her weapon, that's all."

Looking now at the hard-faced, overdressed woman in front of her, Kaye could believe every word. Then Jack was there beside her, his arm possessively around her waist, holding her close, like a shield against trouble.

"Hallo, Elsie," he said. "I've been wondering when you'd show up."

"You might well," Elsie said grimly, "considering how you snatched my child."

"My child, too. It's about time she had a spell living with her father."

"Don't give me that. You think you can just turn up out of the blue and tear my little girl away from me—"

"I didn't have to. You weren't there," Jack pointed out. "You were gallivanting off somewhere with François."

"You swine. You don't care what it did to a mother's heart to come home and find her baby missing."

Jack didn't answer this, but Sam observed maliciously, "It took your mother's heart two months to come after her."

"I've been ill," Elsie shrieked. "I collapsed, I—I was overcome—"

"Even though I left a letter saying she was with me?" Jack said coldly. "Come on, Elsie. You'll have to do better than that. I can take care of our daughter a damned sight better than you can, and you know it. At least with me she's well away from characters like François, not to mention Henri."

"Where *is* the boyfriend?" Sam asked slyly. "Did you bring him along?"

Elsie threw him a look of loathing. "We're having a trial separation," she announced coldly.

Sam cackled. "That's why you've turned up here at last. He's dumped you."

"Shut up, you old fool!" Elsie snapped. "You don't know what you're talking about."

"Is it true, Mom?" Georgy asked. "Have you and François really broken up?"

"For the moment."

"And—Henri?"

"It makes no difference what Henri is or isn't doing," Jack said. "He's not coming within a mile of you, young lady."

Georgy set her chin defiantly. "It's not fair. You've got no right to ruin my life."

Jack groaned. "Is it ruining your life to shield you from a creep?"

"Mom thought he was fine."

"I'm sure she did," Jack retorted grimly. "But that's no recommendation to me."

"Who's Henri?" Paul asked Georgy in an undervoice, while the argument raged around them.

"My boyfriend," she said with an arch smile.

"I'll bet you had lots of them."

"Yes, I did," she said. "Even François gave me the eye. I prefer older men."

"Oh." He looked suitably crestfallen. "Does that mean I don't have a chance?"

"Depends." She gave him a teasing smile.

"On what?"

"On whether you put yourself out to please me."

"Let's dance. Then you can tell me what you like." He took her hand and they ran onto the dance floor.

"And as for you," Elsie said, turning on Kaye suddenly, "standing there like butter wouldn't melt in your mouth. Who are you, when all's said and done?"

"I'm Jack's wife," Kaye said quietly. "Don't underestimate me, Elsie, because you won't find me easy to deal with."

Jack gave her a look of gratitude. "You've had your answer, Elsie," he said. "Perhaps you should go now."

"I'll go when I'm ready. Tell Georgy to come over here. She should be talking to her mother, not dancing with all and sundry."

"Who are you calling all and sundry?" Rhoda demanded, appearing behind Elsie. "That's my son."

"Well, tell him to take his hands off my daughter. She's only fourteen."

"Are you saying my son can't be trusted?" Rhoda snapped.

"I'm saying I know his type. Got a smooth tongue, too handsome for his own good and used to having whatever he wants. And don't pretend you don't know what *that* means."

"I promise you Georgy's safe with my brother." Kaye intervened.

"Your brother?" Elsie turned a jeering look on Jack. "Have you taken on the whole family? That'll cost you before you've finished."

"Here, you watch your tongue," Rhoda snapped, squaring up to Elsie. The two women were oddly alike—both with hard, discontented faces, both overdressed, both slightly tipsy. Each was what the other might have become if she'd taken a different path. Perhaps it was their recognition of like that made them instinctively hostile, like two cats with fur rising on their backs.

"I'm not wasting my time on you," Elsie declared. "But I'm sorry for Jack if he's taken on your crowd. Oh, yes, I've heard the stories. I know how you've all got your claws into him. Jack, you're a fool about people. You always were."

"You should know about that, Elsie," he replied. His voice was deceptively quiet, but through it Kaye could hear the throb of anger, all the more dangerous for being restrained. "Nobody dug her claws in quite as deep as you did."

Elsie didn't bother denying this. "And you fell for it again," she scoffed.

"Don't judge everyone by yourself," he told her. "Kaye's as different from you as one woman could possibly be from another. She married me because she promised a long time ago to come to my aid, no matter what I wanted. Now she's given me her whole life to redeem her promise. That's the kind of woman she is."

Elsie was taken aback, but only for a moment. "Fairy tales! Don't make me laugh."

"That's enough!" Jack said. "Kaye, we should do some more circulating."

He drew her away firmly. She was glad to go with him, away from the other woman's spite. Elsie and Rhoda settled into round two of their slanging match. Let them, Kaye thought. Jack's defense of her was like a song in her heart. Now nothing could hurt her.

Perhaps Jack truly *had* cherished her memory as she'd cherished his. He might have found some other answer to the problem of his daughter. Instead, he'd sought her out, claiming her promise and hurrying her to the altar. Couldn't she dare to hope that some part at least of his heart was hers?

"All right, darling?" Bertie appeared before her, slightly the worse for wear. Kaye regarded him tenderly.

"I'm fine, Grandpa. What about you?"

"Never felt better in my life." He patted his ample stomach. "All I wanted in the world was to see you happy, and now you are, and to know that I helped to make it happen—well."

"Feeling pleased with yourself, you old devil?" Sam asked.

"Yup!" Bertie hiccuped.

"I can see you two were glad to meet again," Kaye said, laughing.

"You could have knocked me down with a feather when I picked up the phone and there was my old partner in crime," Sam confirmed.

"Picked up the phone?" Kaye echoed, puzzled. "When was that?"

"Last week," Sam said. "He'd have called earlier, but it took him that long to discover this address."

Bertie's state of squiffiness had left him happily oblivious to this exchange, but now he belatedly seemed to recognize danger.

"Ah, that's not quite what happened…" he began, casting an uneasy glance at Kaye.

"Yes, it is," Sam insisted. "You said you had to talk to Jack urgently because Kaye's future depended on it, and his office wouldn't tell you where he was, but I said he was in the States, and gave you his number. Don't tell me you've forgotten? Getting daft in your old age! Yes, darling, what can I do for you?''

This last remark was addressed to a luscious middle-aged woman who'd been giving him the eye. He filled her glass and engaged her in a desperate flirtation.

Kaye felt as if Sam's words had turned her to stone. She turned horrified eyes on him. ''That was why Jack came here?'' she whispered. ''*You* fetched him?''

He sighed and gave up. ''I had to stop you marrying Lewis Vane, and Jack was all I could think of. I thought he might find a way to rescue you, and he did. That promise of yours was the perfect way to get you out of Vane's clutches.

''When we left for the church, and there was no sign of Jack, I gave up hope. His plane had been delayed. Still, better late than never, eh? And it all worked out for the best.''

''The best? Oh, Grandpa,'' Kaye said weakly.

''Well, he saved you, didn't he? And now you've married him, and everything's fine.''

Fine. The word had a terrible hollow ring. She'd thought Jack needed her, but it was an act of charity after all. He hadn't even wanted to marry her.

''He was just being kind,'' she whispered.

''Hah!''

Kaye whirled around to see Elsie standing there, hands on hips, regarding her cynically. ''I knew there was something else behind that 'promise' story,'' she said. ''So that's it. Nothing but a plan to leech off him. Well, make the most of it while it lasts, because if I were you, I wouldn't count too much on Jack's 'kindness.' Don't be taken in by his charm, either. It's on the surface. Underneath it there's a calculating brain. Jack does what's good for Jack. He'll use you to get rid of me, and then he'll get rid of you.''

"That's enough out of you," Sam said fiercely. "You know nothing about Jack. Never did."

"I know he's like all men, only more so," Elsie said coarsely. "He'll take what he can get. Oh, he'll sugarcoat it, but it'll happen just the same. Remember that I warned you."

Catching Sam's wrathful eye, she turned away quickly.

"Ignore her, darling," Bertie advised. "She's just being spiteful."

"It's not her," Kaye said softly. "It's knowing that he didn't really want me at all."

She looked across the lawn at where Jack was standing in a small group, swapping jokes. The sound of his laughter carried on the breeze, a rich, delightful sound that stirred her blood. Tears stung her eyes. Only a few moments ago she'd been full of joy and pride, confident of her value to him. Now, one shocking revelation had shown her to herself as a beggar depending on his charity. She wanted to sink with shame.

"Grandpa," she said urgently, "you mustn't tell Jack that we had this talk."

"All right," he said, beginning to understand.

"And Sam—"

"Sam missed half of what we were saying. Too busy making a fool of himself with a woman young enough to be his daughter. Don't worry, darling. I won't interfere. But perhaps you should tell him."

"Never!" she said, so fiercely that his eyes widened.

Somehow she got through the rest of the reception. As the sun began to set, lamps came on in the garden, covering the dancers in a dozen different colored lights. Georgy danced with Paul until Elsie checked her.

"You're not dancing with him again until I've found out a little about him. Come along, young man, you can dance with me."

Paul complied with a good grace, and soon everyone could hear Elsie's shrill laughter as he whirled her about the floor.

"I'm sorry this happened," Jack told Kaye as they waltzed. "But she's Georgy's mother. I can hardly throw her out."

"I don't mind, honestly." Kaye was amazed at how normal her voice sounded, almost as though she wasn't in agony inside.

"Georgy seems very taken with your brother. That's lucky."

"How can you say that? Knowing what you do about him—"

"Oh, if she wanted to marry him I'd show him the door. But if she's flirting with him she isn't pining for Henri. It's okay while I've got them under my eye."

"Jack, look what's happening now," Kaye said urgently.

Elsie had finished dancing with Paul and was engaged in a heated argument with Georgy. The words "That I should live to hear my own daughter speak to me like that—" floated toward them.

"Let's go," Jack said, and headed for the little scene, Kaye's hand clasped in his.

"It's been lovely having you, Elsie," he said untruthfully, "but the party's over."

"She," Elsie said, pointing at Georgy, "is coming with me, right now. She's *mine*."

"You're talking about our daughter, not a piece of property," Jack said in disgust.

"She's mine till she's sixteen, my lawyer says so." Alcohol and thwarted temper had destroyed Elsie's common sense. She'd reached the stage where she barely knew what she was saying.

"I'm not arguing," Jack told her. "I've called you a taxi and it's just arrived."

Elsie's eyes filled with theatrical tears. "Darling—" She tried to appeal to Georgy, but the girl had slipped away while her elders were talking, and was giggling in a corner with Paul.

"In the end, neither of us is going to win," Jack told her, speaking kindly. "Our daughter is growing up, not as fast as she thinks she is, but still fast. She's increasingly going to do what she wants, and never mind us. Neither of us owns her, Elsie."

"I'll take you to court. I'll tell them how you abducted her."

"I'll tell them a few things, too. Do your worst. I've got a wife now, and a stable home to offer my daughter. There's the car. Goodbye."

Elsie's parting shot was for Kaye. "You think you've won, don't you? You may get a shock when you find out just *what* you've won."

Kaye didn't make the mistake of answering this with words. She merely stood close to Jack, letting the picture speak for itself. Elsie's mouth tightened, and she turned away without another word and stormed out.

"We'd—better follow and see she goes," Jack said.

They followed Elsie around to the front and stood watching while the taxi vanished down the drive.

"She'll be back." He sighed. "But for the moment, she's gone. It needed another woman to stand up to her. Thank you—for everything."

The rest of the guests were beginning to leave. Georgy and Paul were still dancing. Rhoda had settled down with a plate piled high with food and seemed about to take root.

"Oh, my, I'm so sleepy," Rhoda said with an exaggerated yawn. "The thought of that journey home is almost too much for me. Our car's broken down— it's always doing that, it's so old—and it's a rough journey by bus."

"I'm sure it is," Jack sympathized, at his most charming. "I'd hate to think of you and Paul having to get yourselves home as late as this."

Rhoda bridled. "Well, it *is* a bit far..." she began archly.

"So I've arranged for Harry to take you home in my car. He's bringing it around the front now. You'll find it very comfortable."

Outmaneuvered, Rhoda tried to come about again. "I wouldn't want to put you to the trouble."

"It's no trouble," he assured her with a smile whose charm masked its determination.

Kaye breathed a sigh of relief. Rhoda usually got what she wanted, and the thought of her imposing on

Jack for the night had been giving her nightmares. But Jack could cope with Rhoda, she realized.

"Why don't you slip away?" Jack murmured to her. "I've got a few goodbyes to make. I won't be long."

He took her face between his hands and kissed her on the lips. It was a beautiful kiss, full of promise for the night to come, and a few hours ago she would have returned it fervently. But now she was full of torment. When he drew back she searched his eyes, longing to find there something that would set her heart at rest. She saw warmth and eagerness, but she wanted much, much more. Heartsick, she turned away and ran upstairs to her room.

The mirror showed her the image of a gorgeous bride, decked out in costly silk and lace, on the "happiest day of her life." Behind her was the huge bed where she would achieve supreme happiness in the arms of her new husband.

Suddenly Kaye couldn't bear that caricature in the mirror. She ripped off the veil and began to tear feverishly at her dress. Her fingers fumbled over the tiny buttons, but she wrenched until they spilled over the floor. She hauled madly at the dress, never caring if it tore in her urgency to get rid of it. But when it was gone, a sense of futility overtook her, and she sank onto the bed, burying her face in her hands.

Bertie had begged Jack's help, and he'd probably frowned, trying to bring her to mind. Instead of remembering her, he'd had to be reminded of her existence. His good nature had made him agree to help out, then her whole family, including herself, had taken advantage of his chivalry to batten on him, just as Elsie had said.

She would gladly have died of shame. All she wanted now was to get far away from here, away from the situation she'd walked into blindly, away from her own stupidity and disillusion.

She couldn't bear the sight of her beautiful nightgown. Its low-cut neck and filmy beauty belonged to the imaginary bride, the one whose husband loved her. But it was all she had to wear, and at last she slipped it over her head. To her despairing eyes it seemed shockingly revealing, and she covered her bosom with her arms.

Tonight she could have claimed Jack and given herself to him in return. Now it was all a heartbreaking mockery.

Chapter Five

A noise outside told her that Jack was coming in, and she quickly turned out the light. As long as he couldn't see her eyes she felt she might be able to face him.

Jack saw her standing in the moonlight by the tall window, and smiled at the pretty sight she made. He was carrying a bottle of champagne and two glasses.

"I thought we'd never get rid of them," he said, coming closer to her. He was wearing a silk dressing gown, loosely tied at the front, revealing his chest, lightly covered with hair. She remembered the other time, on Singleton, when he'd been bare chested, holding her close, and she'd thrilled to be making love with him.

But joy had been snatched away, and tonight it seemed to be happening again.

"Poor Kaye," he said. "It wasn't too much for you, was it?"

"No, I—I'm fine."

"I'm really sorry you had to meet Elsie like that. I'll make sure she doesn't bother you again. Still, now you know why I need you so badly."

"Do you really need me, Jack?" she asked wistfully.

"Can you doubt it? I don't know what I'd have done if I hadn't remembered that you owed me."

"You could have called in that debt at any time," she said in a voice that sounded a little strange to him. "You didn't need to leave it so long."

He hesitated, and she thought she could sense him choosing his words with care. "Things happen when the time is right," he said vaguely. "It was a crisis. I came to you for help."

She wanted to cry out that it wasn't true, that his kindness and chivalry filled her with humiliation. But this would only make things worse. Jack mustn't know that she'd learned the truth. She couldn't bear it.

She should have left it there, but some perverse imp drove her to torment herself. "What made you do it, Jack? After all, that promise was a long time ago."

"Are you saying you didn't mean it?" he asked with a quizzical smile, half turning her by pressing her shoulder.

"No, I meant it. But I don't think it was so important to you that you sought me out all these years later."

"Hey, what is this?" He touched her face. "Honey, you picked the wrong guy for all this soul-searching. I hate analyzing things. Always have. We're here, together. You're beautiful and it's our wedding night. What else matters?''

If only she could feel like that, casting all thoughts aside to live in the moment. But just as his mind rejected analysis, hers insisted on it. ''It matters why you asked me,'' she said desperately. ''You never thought of marriage until the last minute.''

''Oh, that! What the heck! All my best decisions have been made on the spur of the moment. Here.'' He handed her a full champagne glass. ''To us,'' he said, holding up his own glass and touching hers with it.

''To us,'' she replied brightly.

After a moment he lowered his glass. ''You don't sound so keen. What's wrong, Kaye?''

''Nothing. It's been a beautiful wedding. You've saved Paul, you've saved me, you've dealt with Elsie—''

''You dealt with Elsie,'' he interrupted in a strange voice. He was looking at her, puzzled.

''Yes, I did. That's my job, isn't it?''

''Don't say it like that.''

''But I like to believe I'm giving full value for— for—''

''Don't you dare say 'for money,''' Jack broke in, suddenly tense. ''That isn't what this marriage is about.''

''I wish I knew what it *is* about,'' she blurted out.

''I thought we settled that. We need each other.''

''Do we?'' she murmured wistfully.

''It can be a good marriage if we let it, Kaye. Don't you feel that, too?''

What she felt was beyond words. She wanted him

with her whole heart and soul. She wanted him with her body, and never more so than now when he was standing close to her, his chest rising and falling with some emotion that might have been mounting desire. She was suddenly certain that beneath the robe he was naked, and despite her mental anguish the thought caused a stir deep in her flesh. The temptation to forget everything but her love was overwhelming.

Jack reached out and brushed her cheek with a fingertip. It was a touch almost too light to feel, yet it burned her, she craved it so much. A soft sigh escaped her. She wasn't sure whether she'd whispered Jack's name or not, but she thought she had.

The butterfly touch continued down her cheek and across her lips, where it lingered, teasing her, turning her bones to water. A thousand lovings had made Jack a skillful operator who knew how to go carefully, tempting a woman into his arms with subtlety and finesse. The generosity that was the bedrock of his nature made him see things about Kaye that another man might have missed. He saw her shyness and anxiety at this moment, and his tenderest feelings reached out to her. He wasn't in love with her, but he was grateful to her, and her vulnerability touched his heart. In fact, he saw everything about her except what was most important—her love for himself, and her shame at what she'd discovered.

She was beautiful, he realized; her beauty was not blatant, but charming and delicate. The warm silk of her skin was a pleasure, making him want to explore her, enticed further by the elusive perfume that wafted up from between her breasts. He trailed his fingers down farther, along the line of her jaw, her neck, to the hollow of her throat.

Kaye stood quite still, shaken to her roots by what was happening to her. She'd thought she was prepared to face him, but nothing could arm her against the onslaught of feeling that his lightest touch could evoke.

The years fell away. She was eighteen again, hopelessly in love with Jack Masefield, yielding to the sensations he was evoking. This mattered, only this, to be in Jack's arms, feeling his fingers moving gently at the straps of her nightgown, easing them down from her shoulders, following them with kisses.

"I've been thinking of this since that night in the garden," he murmured, his breath scorching her skin. "I couldn't keep my mind on the service this morning, because I was imagining how I was going to undress you—wondering how you'd like it. You do like it—don't you?"

"Yes," she gasped, "yes…"

"And this?"

Her nightgown slipped to the floor, leaving her naked. She heard the soft rustle of silk as he threw aside his dressing gown. Now he was as naked as herself. His whole magnificent body was taut, concentrated on the sensations that possessed him. His touch was still gentle, but growing more insistent, and when he gathered her into his arms to kiss her deeply Kaye's lips parted in readiness.

But in the very same moment she knew she couldn't bear this caricature of love.

"I can't do this."

She didn't know the words had broken from her

until she felt Jack stiffen with shock. A moment ago she'd been aflame with passion, but now it had all drained away, leaving her body cold.

"P-please, Jack," she stammered. "I'd like to talk first."

"All I want to talk about," he said with a groan, "is how lovely you are, and how much I want you. Say you want me, too, Kaye...."

But the world seemed covered in a lurid light, distorting perspectives, turning everything back to front. His impassioned words were only kindly lies, mocking her.

"Jack, wait."

With an effort he forced himself to be still. Kaye could hear his ragged breathing and feel the trembling in his flesh. "Was I going too fast for you?" he asked gently. "I'm sorry."

"Yes, too fast. Not for me, but for you."

"For me?" he echoed quizzically. "Believe me, I know exactly how fast I want to go. I want everything, like we nearly had before—do you remember?" He began kissing her softly again as he spoke.

"Yes," she said raggedly, "but you weren't ill then. Remember your accident. You broke your ribs...."

"I only cracked them, and it was weeks ago," he said, frowning as he began to realize that she was serious. "Kaye, what is this?"

"I—I'm just worried about you—in case you're not really well yet."

He released her. "I see," he said in a strange voice. "How thoughtful of you."

"It's n-not just that," she stammered. "There are

things—things we must talk about first.'' She flinched under the strange, cynical light in his eyes. ''Jack, please go away,'' she blurted out. ''Just for now. I can't explain, not just yet. I need to get my head together—then I'll try to make you understand—''

''I think I do understand,'' he said coolly. ''In fact, the whole thing looks very clear. Don't worry, Kaye. I won't bother you. Good night.''

''Jack—wait—''

But the door had closed behind him. Kaye sat staring at it, shivering with shock.

Her wedding night should have been the happiest of her life, and it had been the worst. A hundred times she relived the sight of Jack's face as he said, ''The whole thing looks very clear.'' He thought she'd frozen him off as soon as she'd got what she wanted. She'd never seen him look so coldly ironic, so close to outright contempt. And how could she blame him?

She would have to give him some explanation the next day. It couldn't be the truth. That would be too dangerously revealing, but she must think of something. She dozed fitfully and awoke in the early hours, lying awake after that to work out what she would say. By the time she had her speech carefully rehearsed it was time to get up.

She found Sam and Bertie already at breakfast, in a sun-filled room overlooking the garden. There was nobody else there, but after a moment Georgy bounced in and greeted her.

''Poor Dad,'' she said. ''He's had Alex on the phone. Alex is the designer of the boat, and he's in a terrible state, sure that everything's going to go wrong.

Dad calmed him down, but when Alex got here he was in a state again, so Dad's calming him down all over again.''

"Who calms Jack down?" Bertie asked between mouthfuls of ham.

"Nobody needs to," Sam declared. "Nothing gets to Jack. Nerves of steel. Gets it from me."

Georgy hooted with laughter. "What about that time you bought those luxury exercise bikes, and put too many zeros on the order, and it blew a hole in the budget and nobody could move for bikes, and you panicked—"

"I did no such thing," Sam asserted. "I rose loftily above the whole affair."

"Only because Dad sorted it out for you," Georgy said, tucking in. "Like he always does."

"Hey, a bit of respect, young lady."

The conversation became an amiable slanging match. Kaye had no appetite, but she forced herself to take some grapefruit and coffee, glad that nobody was looking at her. She wasn't sure whether to be relieved or sorry that today's commotion would prevent any intimate talk between her and Jack.

At last she heard his study door open. Jack appeared, his arm around a small, thin man with a worried expression.

"That's enough talking," he was saying. "Come to breakfast and meet my wife."

He reached out a hand to Kaye. Now she could see his eyes. And they gave her a shock.

There was nothing there: no anger, no question, no awareness, even. Jack was smiling and friendly, but it was the general goodwill he would have shown a stranger. An outsider, watching him make the introductions, would have said that here was a man who had an affectionate, untroubled relationship with his wife. Only his eyes revealed that he was keeping her at an emotional distance.

It was like that for the rest of the day, with no time for any awkwardness between the bride and groom. The race was taking up everyone's time and attention, and the hours were packed with preparations. When night came, Jack stayed up working until the early hours.

At one in the morning Kaye slipped downstairs and into the study. Jack was just putting down the phone.

"Shouldn't you be getting some sleep?" she ventured. "You'll be in no state to race a boat."

"I can do without sleep," he said, leaning back in his chair and stretching.

"But are you well enough to be doing this?" she asked worriedly. "You came out of hospital so recently, and it was much sooner than the doctors wanted you to go."

"Doctors," he said witheringly. "What do they know?"

"They knew you had a concussion and two cracked ribs."

"From which I've completely recovered, as I told you once before." Jack's voice held a faint, ironic edge that made her flinch.

"Can't you wait a little longer before you get back into that boat?" she pleaded.

"No. Time's running out. I have an option that expires in a few days and there are other people interested. Before I can decide, I have to know why I crashed. Was it my fault, or the boat's?''

"So what are you going to do? Crash again, in order to find out?'' she demanded indignantly.

"If that's what it takes,'' he said, getting up and strolling across the floor.

"Jack, please—''

"Hey, have I married a nag?'' He slipped an arm around her shoulder.

"Of course not, but—''

"Good, I was getting worried.''

His tone was amiable, but the arm around her was firmly urging her out the door. His friendly smile gave nothing away. Kaye found herself outside the study, with Jack blocking the way in.

"Go and get some beauty sleep,'' he said. ''There'll be cameras on you tomorrow. Night.''

"Good night,'' she said to the closed door.

She shivered. Jack couldn't have spelled out the terms of their relationship more clearly if he'd said it in words. She was his wife. She could share his home, walk beside him and smile in the face of the world. But she had no influence with him. None at all.

Next morning saw an early start for Dover, by helicopter. Georgy was in high spirits. Her father's villainy in separating her from Henri and forcing her to wear the school uniform was forgotten in the excitement of the occasion.

"I love it when Dad does things like this,'' she confided to Kaye. "There'll be reporters and television crews there, and they always trot out a model or two to give him a big kiss—'' She checked herself, adding hastily, ''I expect they'll skip that bit this time.''

''They'd better,'' Jack said with a laugh. ''I've gone off being kissed by models ever since one of them turned out to be a private detective serving me with a summons. I'd evaded it really well until then, but they got me.''

''A summons?'' Kaye echoed.

''Nothing serious. I was only a witness, but I didn't want to be. It would have involved admitting whose company I'd been in at the time....'' He cleared his throat. ''It was a question of a lady's reputation, and let's talk about something else.''

At last they saw the gleam of the sea, and Dover was in sight. Soon after, they landed, to be met by Charlie Daker, Jack's director of publicity. He was a middle-aged man with rapidly thinning sandy hair, clearly a wizard at his job.

A fleet of cars was ready on the tarmac to carry everyone the short distance to the shore, where a band was playing, flags were flying and stands had been set up for spectators. There were also two enormous screens to receive pictures by satellite when the boats were out of sight.

''Stick close by me,'' Jack said to Kaye, putting an arm around her waist and riveting her to his side. ''Defend me from marauding women.''

She smiled, determined to put her own concerns aside and do nothing that might spoil his day. It was clear that Jack was in his element, enjoying the spotlight, caught up in the thrill of the danger that was meat and drink to him.

The two powerboats were already in the water, each

long and sleek, built for speed. The sight of them gave Kaye a slight shock. "Jack, it's dangerous," she whispered.

"No way! Piece of cake," he said cheerfully. "Don't worry. I've driven that thing a hundred times and I'm still here. I've got to go now. Charlie will look after you."

"Be careful," she said, holding on to him impulsively.

"Hey, c'mon! I'm indestructible." He gave her his most mischievous grin. "Either that or you'll be a rich widow."

"Don't even joke about it," she whispered. "Jack—"

"Bye, sweetheart. Go and enjoy yourself."

He kissed her cheek and strode off to shake hands with the other driver, who was advancing to meet him. Kaye had no choice but to join the rest as they went inside to have a champagne lunch.

She tried to put her fears aside and concentrate on keeping the champagne out of Georgy's reach. Nobody else seemed troubled for Jack's safety, but Sam touched her arm gently and said, "Don't worry, darling. The gremlins have never got him yet."

"They've come pretty close," she reminded him.

"But he's still here," Sam pointed out unarguably.

"He made a joke about being a rich widow. I wish he hadn't."

"Better than being a poor one," Sam said impishly.

"Oh, you're as impossible as he is," she said crossly, and he roared with laughter.

At last it was time to take their places in the ferry. When everyone was aboard, the big boat began to move out to sea, until Dover was out of sight. Now they were dependent on the giant screen that had been set up on deck, and which clearly showed what was happening in the port behind them.

The two drivers appeared, dressed in sleek water-proof suits—red for Jack, blue for the other driver—and shook hands, to cheers. Jack waved before putting on his helmet and climbing into the cockpit of his boat, sliding so far down that he almost vanished. Kaye could just see his red helmet through the thick windscreen that went all around him.

Both boats started up, roared out of the port and were soon visible from the ferry. The bay was full of small launches, and for the first few minutes the two powerboats wove among them, giving a display of speed and maneuvering on their way to the official starting line. But at last the signal came and they raced over the line together.

Without the screen Kaye couldn't have made out what Jack was doing. Two sets of buoys had been laid out in matching patterns, and the two boats swerved away from each other to weave their way around these a safe distance apart.

Kaye knew nothing about this sport, but even she could see that Jack was pushing the boat to the limit. Every turn was as tight as he could make it, and her heart was in her mouth as she watched him. The other driver was taking the turns wider, losing time.

Plainly she was the only one who was worried. Everyone else took it for granted that Jack was invincible. The boat's designer hung over the rail with her, watching every move. "He's testing that boat to destruction," he breathed.

His satisfied tone riled Kaye and she turned on him. "Let's hope for your sake that isn't true," she snapped. "Otherwise you'll have me to deal with."

He backed off at something in her eyes. "Just a figure of speech," he said hastily.

The only other person who seemed troubled was a tall, dark man who watched every move obsessively through binoculars, drawing in a sharp breath each time Jack took a risk, and clenching his fingers on the rail. Kaye began to feel kindly toward him.

"I don't think we've met," she said. "I'm Jack's wife."

He shook hands. "I'm George Fernham," he said, "Jack's business manager. To be honest, I was hoping you'd manage to talk him out of this. Of course, his high profile is good for the company, but not if he kills himself."

"The company," Kaye echoed, feeling chilled again.

"If Jack goes down the chute so does everything," Fernham said gloomily. "The insurance companies won't touch him, you know. They say he's mad."

Kaye turned angrily away. Charlie came after her. "Don't get upset," he advised her cheerily.

"Someone needs to," she said indignantly. "You're all heartless."

"Not heartless. Just used to Jack always coming through. Nothing can touch him. You'll see."

The boats had swept out of sight again and everyone's attention was focused on the screen. Grinding her nails into her palm, Kaye watched as they swung back in line and headed for home.

"They'll be in sight in about ten minutes," Charlie

said. He was frowning a little. "Jack's lost his lead. I thought he'd be well ahead by this time. So did he, by the way he's driving."

"What do you mean?" Kaye asked anxiously.

"He's getting frustrated. You can see it in little things."

It would soon be over, she thought, trying to take comfort from that. At last the boats appeared on the horizon and everyone crowded to the rail as they began the final maneuvers, swinging tightly around the buoys, both seeking every last inch of advantage. The finish line was in sight.

"One more turn," Georgy said excitedly. "Dad's ahead."

"Only just," Charlie muttered. "If I know Jack, that won't be good enough."

"But it's not really a race, is it?" Kaye asked. "Surely the idea is to test the boat?"

"Officially," Charlie said with a grin. "But Jack has to win. Anything less just isn't good enough— *My God!*"

The exclamation was torn from him at the sight of Jack taking the final turn at a sharp angle. Either he miscalculated or the boat wasn't built for it, for he clipped the buoy so lightly that at first the spectators thought he'd gotten away with it. But suddenly the boat reared up into the air and twisted violently.

Somebody screamed, and Kaye realized that it was her. The boat spun wildly before hitting the water again with a crash, swinging around, thundering against the buoy and disintegrating. Kaye buried her face in her hands.

When she looked up again Jack was already being

pulled out of the water by the other driver, who'd turned back and dived in. He held him up until the ferry could reach them. Terrified, Kaye watched for any sign of life, but Jack never moved.

He was dead. He should never have made that joke about her being a rich widow. It was bad luck. Her legs had turned to jelly, but somehow she managed to move them along the deck to where he was being lifted aboard. They laid him down and someone removed his helmet. His hair was wet and tousled and there was blood running down his face.

"Jack," she whispered, kneeling beside him. "Jack...open your eyes—*please*." He didn't respond, and she grew frantic. "I can't lose you like this," she pleaded, "not after all these years—when I thought—I hoped—you can't leave me now—I won't let you."

To lose him would be an agony, but almost as bad was the thought that he might die thinking she had rejected him, never dreaming of her true feelings.

"I love you," she whispered, close to his ear. "I've always loved you. I'm sorry about our wedding night, but even that was because I love you—if only you could understand...."

He gave a faint groan, and she gripped his hand, breathless with hope. The next moment he opened his eyes, looking straight at her. She tried to read his expression, to know whether he'd heard her. His first words would tell her what her heart longed to know....

"Kaye—?"

"Yes?" she breathed.

"Help me up—" He tried to reach for her and fell back.

"Keep still," Charlie urged. "We'll get you into an ambulance as soon as we reach the shore."

"Where's Alex?" Jack demanded in a husky voice.

The little designer was there, almost hysterical. "I'm sorry," he kept saying, "I'm so sorry—I can't think what—"

"Hush up and listen," Jack commanded. "It's a terrific boat. I want it. Get the papers ready for me to sign."

"Jack!" Kaye exclaimed in horror. "It nearly killed you."

"That was my own fault. Alex, do it."

"Oh, God!" Kaye raged, driven beyond endurance. "Is that all you can think of?"

Jack began to heave and choke. When he could speak again he said, "My own fault—took that last turn too fast—wonderful boat—"

His eyes closed again. He was dreadfully pale.

"Daddy!" Georgy cried. Her sophisticated pose had vanished and she looked around frantically for comfort. Kaye took the girl into her arms and they clung together.

"It's all right," she said fiercely. "I'm sure it isn't too serious."

"Then why are you crying?" Georgy wept.

"I'm not—not really—oh, Georgy!" She fought to control her tears, but they flowed anyway.

The ambulance was waiting on the shore, and in minutes Jack was being lifted into it and hurriedly attached to drips.

"We've got room for one," the paramedic said.

"Wait for Kaye," Sam called.

"Me, too," Georgy begged.

"No, darling, Kaye's his wife," Sam said, slipping his arm around Georgy's shoulder. "We'll follow right behind in the car."

"Let Georgy go," Kaye said bleakly.

Georgy gave her a swift hug of gratitude and scurried into the ambulance. Kaye tried not to see the puzzled stares of those around her. "She's known him all her life," she said to Sam. "I'm really—just an outsider."

She said the last words so softly that Sam had to strain to hear, and she turned quickly away before he could ask.

"Did you hear that?" Sam demanded of Bertie.

"I sure did. And I don't like it."

Charlie drove them to the local hospital. With a discretion nobody would have expected from their riotous behavior, the two old men stayed silent. Bertie held Kaye's hand tightly. Sam patted her knee before relapsing into a corner. He suddenly looked his full age, and Kaye forgot her own feelings to say, "He *has* been like this before, hasn't he, Sam? And come through it."

"Lots of times," he declared robustly, and blew his nose.

Charlie tried to keep close to the ambulance, but they were delayed by a traffic light, and by the time they moved again the ambulance was well ahead.

As soon as the ambulance reached the hospital Georgy jumped down and looked around for the car but, seeing no sign of it, she followed the trolley, bearing her father, inside.

"Shouldn't he have come round?" she asked anxiously as the paramedics handed over to a doctor.

"I think he's waking now," the doctor said.

Jack was stirring. "Kaye?" he whispered.

"No, Daddy, it's me."

"Kaye?" He opened his eyes, his gaze flickering from side to side. "Kaye?"

"She'll be here in a minute," Georgy said. "There was only room for one of us."

"Oh, yes—of course. Hallo, darling."

He drifted into unconsciousness again as he was wheeled away. As the swing doors closed on the trolley, Kaye and the two old men appeared at the other end of the corridor. Sam and Bertie were fulminating after an encounter with the press as they arrived.

"Damned vultures!" Bertie was saying.

Kaye had herself fully under control again. Whatever her feelings, nobody would be allowed to suspect them. She'd pushed her way through the press with a set face, and now all her concern was to learn Jack's fate and look after Georgy.

"Is he still unconscious?" she asked the girl.

"He woke for a moment, but the doctor took him away at once."

Kaye tried to shut down her imagination. It was useless to think the worst. But she was tormented by the way she'd rejected Jack on grounds that seemed foolish now, when he might be dying.

But then came the other memory, herself kneeling beside him, telling him of her love, seeing his eyes open, hoping he would respond to her words. And he'd thought only of the boat. He probably hadn't even heard her, but if he had, he wasn't interested.

It might have been one hour or five when the swing doors opened and the doctor returned. The four people sitting there looked up quickly, their eyes fixed on his face, which wore, incredibly, a grin.

"He's fitter than I am," he said. "At least, according to him."

"You mean he's all right?" Kaye breathed.

"Three broken ribs, a chipped bone in his shoulder, and mild concussion!"

"I told you!" Sam roared. "Like last time. Just like last time."

He went on repeating this as though it was some kind of personal triumph. Kaye was almost faint with relief.

They were allowed into Jack's room for a few minutes. He was lying propped up against pillows, looking weary, but awake.

"Told you I'm indestructible," he said with the ghost of a grin. "Oh, ye of little faith!"

"Whaddaya mean?" Sam demanded. "I always knew I couldn't get rid of you. Been trying since the day you were born."

Jack managed to laugh and return Georgy's hug. "I want to be alone with Kaye," he said huskily.

The others made their way to the door. When it had closed behind them Jack beckoned for Kaye to come to the bed.

"Something really important to say to you—haven't got much voice left. Listen carefully."

She nodded, her heart beating faster with hope.

"About Georgy—I'll be here a few days, and while I'm off the scene Elsie may make a move. Watch out for that. Don't let Georgy out of your sight. Sam will help, but he's a bit—erratic. You'll have to be fully responsible. Can you do that?''

She took a deep breath, fighting not to let her disappointment show. She'd hoped so much that Jack's words would be something personal, intimate even. But she'd forgotten the reality of their marriage.

''I can do it,'' she told him. ''I'll keep Georgy safe for you.''

''Thanks. I know I can rely on you.'' His eyes on her were dark and puzzled.

''What is it, Jack?''

''Did I come round when I was on the boat?''

''Just for a moment.''

''I thought so, but it's so vague…I can't remember. There was something important—oh, yes—''

''Yes?'' She could hardly speak.

''Alex. I told him I want that boat. Talk to Mary— tell her to contact him and make sure he understood. Get the paperwork going—I don't want to lose this.…''

''Of course,'' Kaye said in a colorless voice. ''Is that all you wanted to say to me?''

''Yes, except…'' He reached out his hand and she took it. ''I guess you were right. Maybe I'll listen to you another time.''

''Maybe,'' she said in a shaky voice, squeezing his hand. ''But I'm not counting on it.''

''Getting to know me, huh?''

''A little.'' She took a sudden breath. ''Jack, I—''

''My head's aching like the devil. I think I'll sleep now.''

''Yes, of course.''

She went quietly to the door and looked back. His eyes were already closed.

Chapter Six

Next day an ambulance conveyed Jack to a hospital near Maple Lodge, and two days later he was home. As before, he discharged himself in the teeth of his doctors' objections.

"I've promised not to do anything strenuous," he told his family, "and of course I shall feel honor bound to keep my promise." He said this with an unnaturally straight face, and Bertie and Sam obliged on cue by roaring with laughter. "I don't know what's the matter with you two," he said with a defiant grin. "I'm a man of my word."

"Sure you are," Sam agreed at once.

"And to prove it, I'm going to sleep downstairs in the study for a while. It'll save dragging my old bones up the stairs."

He didn't look at Kaye while he said this. Mindful

of the curious eyes of the others, she smiled and said, "I'll bet you also promised not to work too hard. No prizes for guessing if you're going to keep that one."

"Certainly I shall keep it," he replied with offended dignity. "When I've answered my letters, returned phone calls, read reports, signed whatever needs signing, negotiated with the bank and cleared my In tray, I shall rest."

In days he was going about his business as if nothing had happened. He took his family out to a riotous lunch to celebrate his "recovery" and also "something else" about which he was determinedly mysterious. The answer was revealed when they returned home to find a new car gleaming in the sunlight outside the front door.

"Your wedding present," he said, smiling at Kaye.

The car was pale blue, sleek and elegant, and she loved it at first sight.

"Jack," she breathed, thrilled. "I never expected—"

"As long as you like it."

"Like it..." The next moment she yielded to her impulse and threw her arms about his neck, kissing him eagerly. He laughed and kissed her back, the very picture of an affectionate husband. Georgy bounced about, applauding. Sam and Bertie were loud in their praise. Sam opened the door and showed Kaye everything, as though she'd never seen a car before. It was a happy moment, but it would have been far sweeter if Jack had given it to her when they were alone.

He didn't even wait but limped back into the house while Sam was still droning on. Kaye found him in his study a few minutes later, looking drawn and rubbing his shoulder.

"You've overdone it," she said anxiously.

"Quit sounding like Sam," he said amiably. "I don't know which of you is more of an old woman."

"Jack, it's a lovely car. Thank you so much for thinking of me—"

"You'll need a car if you're going to chauffeur Georgy around, and I can't always spare Harry," he said smoothly. "You'll find it light and easy to drive. I told him to watch out for that."

"Harry chose it?"

"He's the expert. There aren't many men I'd trust with my wife and daughter's safety, and I've been a bit tied up." He ruefully indicated his shoulder.

"Yes, of course. It's just that… Thank you."

"As long as you're pleased."

"Jack, how much longer are you going to sleep down here? I'm sure you could—"

"The couch is very comfortable, and the stairs still give me some trouble. Leave it to time, Kaye." While she stood irresolute, he smiled at her again. The sight of that blank smile brought back the words he'd spoken long ago.

I wonder sometimes if giving people things isn't really a way of giving them nothing.

Jack had been speaking about himself, but she hadn't believed him. Until now.

"Why don't you go and try out the car?" he asked. And if he'd said, "Run away and play with your toys," he couldn't have made his meaning plainer.

She spent the afternoon getting the feel of the vehicle. It was perfect, and if there had been anything personal about the gift she would have been completely happy.

Jack didn't join the family for supper, and Sam explained that he was spending the evening on the phone to foreign contacts. When it was time for bed she went in to say good-night, and Jack blew her a kiss from a great distance.

"Come and have a nightcap," Sam called as she went out of the study.

He was alone in the front room. As he pressed her favorite sherry into her hand, Kaye thanked him and joined him on the sofa. She was reluctant to go upstairs to her lonely room, and it was pleasant to sit here with Sam. By now she was almost as fond of him as of Bertie.

"He's doing too much," Sam said with a sigh.

"I know. But I can't stop him. Can you?"

"Me? Jack hasn't listened to me since he took over our first shop years ago and stopped it going under— that is, when I took him into partnership and showed him the secrets of... Oh, what the hell! You know what I mean."

"Yes," she said with a fond smile.

"He's always gone his own way, no matter what anybody thought. Oh, he'll do it nicely. He's got the charm of the devil—"

"I think that's in the genes, too," Kaye said, raising her glass to him.

"That's one thing I did show him," Sam said brightly. "How to sugarcoat it, so's you don't see what's really happening until it's too late. 'Course, he does it to me now." He made a face. "I wonder sometimes what would have happened if Jack's mother was still with us.''

''Did she die long ago?''

''She ain't dead. Leastways, I don't think so. She left when he was twelve. Never heard from her again.''

''His mother abandoned him when he was that young?'' Kaye echoed, horrified.

''That's right. Not a backward glance for either of us. Her new man didn't want to be bothered with a child.''

''Poor Jack, that must have devastated him.''

''It did, but you wouldn't have known it. On the surface he coped wonderfully, always cheerful and smiling. But I used to hear him crying at night when he was in bed. I'd go in to him, and we'd talk, and sometimes he'd let me get close. Other times he'd swear he hadn't been crying, and everything was fine. Then he'd make a joke to turn the subject. Or he'd try to comfort me.

''When he met Elsie I could see trouble coming from the start. He was only twenty-one and she's eight years older, but he was infatuated with her. He'd already made his first fortune, and she set out to get him. She was an actress in those days, and she sure put on the right act.

''When she got pregnant Jack didn't think twice. Marriage. I tried to warn him against her, but once Jack's made up his mind, people tend to do what he says.''

''Yes,'' Kaye agreed with a little smile.

''Well, I guess you've discovered that. Of course,

the marriage was a disaster. She was his mother all over again, walked out for a new man.''

''But she didn't abandon her child.''

Sam snorted. ''She would have done if it had suited her. But Jack loved that little girl. He used to rush home to play with her before she went to bed, and he was always buying her silly presents—all that sentimental stuff, you know.

''So taking Georgy gave Elsie a hold over Jack. She was a weapon, that's all. He made Elsie a generous settlement—far more than she deserved after the way she acted—and she's gone on screwing money out of him ever since.''

''However did he manage not to become bitter?'' Kaye wondered.

''He drew back into himself instead,'' Sam said seriously. ''You might not think it, the way he laughs and charms everyone, but that's partly a way of keeping people off his pitch. He's got it to a fine art now. Inside, even I'm not sure who he is anymore, except that he doesn't trust anyone, especially women. He expects folk to disappoint him, and when they do he doesn't get mad, he just shrugs and moves on.''

He might have added that it was all part of a pattern that Jack should have married in the way he did. Choosing a woman who was almost a stranger, hustling her to the altar with no words of love asked or given, left him feeling in control, and therefore safe.

But Sam said none of this because, like his son, he wasn't strong on analysis. What he'd managed to tell Kaye so far represented an heroic effort.

''I've disappointed him,'' Kaye said slowly.

''I don't believe that. I don't know what's wrong

between you two, and I'm not prying. But if ever I
saw the right woman for Jack, you're the one. By
'right' I mean someone who can understand the way
he is, and make allowances for it, and keep holding
on until it works.

"Mostly that'll be down to you. You mustn't expect
Jack to know what you're thinking. He's not the most
subtle of men, and in some ways he ain't clever."

"Not clever?" Kaye echoed in astonishment.

"Oh, he's brilliant about *things*. He can juggle fig-
ures like balls in the air, and he's only got to lay his
hand on an engine to know what it can do to the thou-
sandth rev. But people—" Sam shook his head de-
spairingly. "He's just dumb about what makes them
tick. Guess he gets that from me," he added after a
moment.

"I think you understand plenty," Kaye said.

"Mostly what I find out from Bertie," Sam said
significantly.

"Grandpa's got a big mouth." Kaye sighed.

"True. And he's a fool. But not such a fool as my
son."

"Sam, you won't—"

"What do you take me for? There's things Jack's
got to find out for himself. But don't let him take too
long. Kick him in the rear now and then. Do him a
power of good."

They went upstairs together, and at her door Sam
kissed her cheek warmly. "Don't give up, darling,"
he said. "You're Jack's last chance."

Jack listened to the murmur of Sam's and Kaye's
voices in the hall, then their footsteps going upstairs,

and then the house growing quiet around him. Soon everyone would be asleep—everyone except himself.

All his life he'd needed little sleep, but these days he hardly had any. The couch was comfortable enough, but it couldn't stop his thoughts following Kaye into her room. His mind would persist in seeing her remove her clothes, gradually revealing the slender body that had twice so nearly been his. There was an abyss between them that he couldn't cross, yet he could clearly see every beautiful, tormenting detail.

For years he'd cheerfully passed his time with a succession of well-endowed beauties who gave and took on an equal basis, knowing his limited needs, happy to satisfy them in return for a good time. Jack was a man who knew how to give a woman a good time, and until now he'd had no complaints.

Kaye was entirely different from these women, both spiritually and physically, but therein lay her very attraction. Her delicate loveliness was a teasing incitement. It wasn't merely the soft roundness of her body and the grace of her movements. It was the way she turned her head, and the light in her eyes. He envied those on whom that light fell. Once it had fallen on him, but on his wedding night the light had been switched off, and he still didn't know why.

It was misery to want her so fiercely and know that she didn't want him. But the greater pain was feeling that he'd been deceived in her. This woman, whom his instincts had told him was better than all the others, had proved herself worse, cheating on their bargain by rejecting him as soon as the ring was on her finger. As behavior it was devious and dishonest. And Jack prized honesty. Some of his business dealings might sail close to the wind, but only with others like himself, who knew the risks. In his personal relationships he was straighter than most men.

His pride revolted from the thought of demanding an explanation from Kaye. He'd never yet begged for a place in a woman's bed, and he wasn't going to start with his own wife.

Sometimes, tossing and turning in the small hours, he was sure he knew the answer. There was another man who held her heart, and the thought of him had put up a barrier against her husband.

Then he would awake and in the light of day he would recognize this theory for the nonsense that it was. Kaye was incapable of such deceit.

That was almost the worst pain of all: that in the midst of everything, his original belief in her flowered untouched.

After a few more days he moved back upstairs to his own room. Even his ingenuity couldn't stretch his sojourn on the couch beyond this point, and he was aware that the household was beginning to regard him curiously.

All except Kaye. Gradually it was borne in on Jack that Kaye didn't look at him at all if she could help it. She grew more distant from him by the hour, and the more remote she was the more she tormented him.

He tried not to let this show. He couldn't go near her without wanting to touch her, so he avoided going near at all. He was afraid of the temptation to caress her cheek or lay his hand over hers. He was even more afraid of the fierce physical longing that would possess him without warning. It was a weakness, and one that he couldn't risk.

He was well enough, now, to leave the house. He began spending long hours in his London office, returning as late as possible.

It was time for Georgy to return to school. She complained about this, but in a halfhearted manner that suggested she'd already sized up the strength of the opposition. Aylesbury Lodge was an excellent establishment with an enviable academic record, but it insisted on dressing its pupils alike. The summer uniform was a cotton dress of white-and-mauve check, designed on the principle that its wearers were sexless children. It naturally found no favor with Georgy.

"If Henri sees me in this I'll die. I'll just die," she moaned.

"Then we'll have to hope that he doesn't show up," Kaye replied briskly. "Luckily there's no sign of him."

Georgy flung her a look of loathing, which Kaye pretended not to see. She was more aware of Jack, hiding his grins behind his newspaper. He didn't hide them well enough.

"And you're no help," Georgy informed him. "You don't care if Kaye ruins my life."

"That's right, I don't," he agreed affably. "I'm even going to help her ruin it by driving you to school and making sure you get there."

Georgy fulminated in silence, while attacking her breakfast with youthful heartiness. "Henri's not the only pebble on the beach," she said stormily at last.

"I'll tell him that, if I see him," Kaye observed cheerfully.

"What about Paul? Suppose he calls and sees me in this?"

"I hope he does," Kaye said firmly. "It'll remind him that you're only fourteen."

Kaye had heard nothing from Paul for a few weeks. When she called, Rhoda answered to say that "poor Paul" was taking a little vacation in Italy to recover from the strain he'd been under.

He telephoned her at last, sounding more cheerful than he had since before his trouble with Lewis. "Hi, sis! Long time, no see!"

"How was Italy?"

"Fantastico! I'll tell you all about it when we meet."

"All right, I'll buy you lunch. You choose where."

He named an expensive Italian restaurant in central London, explaining his choice with, "My heart's still in Italy."

Kaye set out, looking forward to the meeting with the brother who, despite everything, retained a hold on her heart.

Paul was late arriving, but then he swaggered in like a lord of creation, fully knowing the attention he was attracting. Not many young men were as beautiful as Paul. His clothes were stylish and looked brand-new.

"Not late, am I?" he asked, kissing her cheek.

"Not more than I expected," she said cheerfully.

The wine waiter appeared. Kaye left the choice to Paul, meaning to drink nothing but mineral water.

"White with the pasta, I think," he said with the air of an expert, "and red to follow."

He made a great performance over the selection of food, peppering his words with Italian phrases. Finally he chose the most expensive dishes on the menu and returned it with a confident air that made the waiter bow low.

"How long have you been back?" Kaye asked.

"A week, and I wish I'd stayed away. You should hear the way Mom goes on. The house is very empty without you. It makes me realize how you used to keep her off my back. I never appreciated you enough, sis."

There was a warm note in his voice that told her he was angling for something. Strangely, it didn't affect her as much as it once had. She saw him a little more clearly now. Or perhaps she'd always seen him clearly, but had still clung to him as someone to love. Now her love for Jack filled her life, even if it wasn't returned.

"You shouldn't criticize Mom," she said. "I expect she paid for those clothes you're wearing."

"There you're wrong. I've got a new credit card," he said loftily. "Actually, I needed some new clothes for my new job. I had a chance to do some modeling. I wanted to make a good impression, so I kitted myself out."

"Modeling," Kaye exclaimed in delight. "But that's wonderful. Did they offer you anything?"

"Yes, a couple of days' work."

For a moment she basked in a vision of Paul doing the only work for which he was really qualified, looking pretty. He could make decent money and be a success in spite of everything. But his next words smashed the illusion.

"It didn't work out. So I told them to chuck it."

"You what? Oh, Paul…"

"Don't start sounding like Mom," he said petulantly.

"But why?"

"Artistic differences."

"What really happened?"

"That's right, show you trust me. Look, I was only five minutes late, okay? It wasn't my fault. Anyway, it's no big deal. Something will turn up."

Despite his claims of destitution, Paul ate and drank like a prince, doing everything with a flourish and conducting a rattling monologue. Kaye laughed despite herself, for Paul was delightful in this mood.

"I'm so glad things worked out well for you," he said warmly. "If ever anyone deserved to land on her feet, it's you."

"Thank you, darling."

"Jack's a great guy, and I'll bet he doesn't keep you short."

"Are you angling for a loan?"

"Not a loan exactly," he said with his sweetest smile. "It's just that—well, there's this."

He took out a paper that she recognized as a credit card statement, and slid it across the table toward her. Kaye's eyes widened. The bill was over two thousand pounds, all run up in Italy.

"Please, Kaye, just this month's payment. I'm not asking you to pay it all—although if you felt you could, that would be wonderful—but just one month…"

Kaye steeled herself. "No, Paul. I can't ask Jack for any more. He gives me so much—and he got you off Lewis Vane's hook."

"But need you tell him? I don't suppose he asks how you spend every penny?"

Paul's instinct was spot on. Jack made her a large allowance and asked no questions. But she found this largesse more crushing than pleasant, as it implied indifference. "I can't spend his money like this without telling him," she said, trying to sound firm.

"But surely it's your money too, now, isn't it? I'll bet that's what he'd say."

"Yes, he would, and it's just because he trusts me that I won't do this." She pushed the statement back across the table. "I'm sorry, Paul."

He scowled for a moment, then took it back with a shrug. After that they made small talk in a halfhearted way until it was time to go.

Paul raised his eyes at her sleek new car, but Kaye was too busy opening the door to notice the wry twist of his lips. She offered him a lift home and he sat in thoughtful silence until she pulled in to a gas station.

"I'd better fill up here," she said, switching off the engine and taking her purse out of her bag. "I won't be a moment."

Left alone, Paul regarded the bag she'd left on the floor. It had a gold clasp and smelled deliciously of real leather. He reckoned it had probably cost at least enough to pay this month's installment on his card. Life just wasn't fair!

Kaye was paying for the gas, standing with her back to him. Moving quickly, Paul took the statement out of his jacket and slipped it into her bag, pushing it right down out of sight. When Kaye returned he was leaning out of the car window, awaiting her with an expectant smile.

She dropped him off and drove home, brooding about a plan she was hatching. For once Jack was at home, and she found him alone.

"Are you busy?" she asked. "Or can we talk?"

She thought a slight look of alarm flickered over his face, but it was replaced instantly by an amiable smile that gave nothing away. "Of course. Been out socializing?"

"Only with Paul."

"How is he?"

"Same old Paul."

"You're not letting him leech off you, are you, Kaye?"

"Of course not," she said quickly. For a moment she almost confided in him about Paul's request and her refusal, but decided against it. She had no idea that her mobile face registered every thought, and that her indecision was obvious to Jack.

"Did you want to talk to me about Paul?" he asked.

"No, something else. Now Georgy's gone back to school, I need something to do during the day."

"Get a job, you mean?" he asked, frowning.

"Sort of. Not a paid job. There's a little nursery school near Aylesbury Lodge. It's for children with disabilities, and they need volunteers. I've talked to them, and when they heard I was a trained infant teacher they nearly fell on me. I could make my own hours, go there while Georgy's at school, and still be ready to collect her. When the summer vacation comes, I can take a break."

She was unaware that her eagerness had brought a glow to her face, and that she was making urgent gestures. Jack regarded her quizzically, and took one of her hands in his.

"You won't be happy unless you do this, will you?" he asked.

"I can't just waft around spending money, Jack."

"Don't you like spending money?"

"It was lovely at first, but I've run out of ideas." She gave an awkward laugh. "It's boring."

He looked at her for a moment, a strange look in his eyes, then unexpectedly raised her hand and brushed it against his cheek. "You're a remarkable woman," he said softly.

A sweet warmth began to creep through her. He hadn't spoken to her in that tone since before their disastrous wedding night. She could hardly believe that she'd made a breakthrough when she was almost in despair.

"Jack..." she said softly.

Before he could reply they were interrupted by the sound of two voices raised in riotous argument outside Jack's door.

"It's an art," Sam was bellowing. "You just need the right touch on the throttle."

Bertie's voice followed, mumbling inaudibly until he roared, "To blazes with the damned throttle!"

"If you'd done what I told you instead of arguing all the time," Sam yelled, "you wouldn't have fallen off."

"I forgot," Jack groaned. "Sam's been teaching Bertie to ride his motorbike."

"*What?*" Kaye jumped up and hurried to the door, moving so fast that she knocked over her bag. Oblivious, she rushed out to where Bertie was sitting down, rubbing his leg and protesting loudly about the iniquity of his companion and all machines.

Grinning, Jack leaned down to pick up the bag and retrieve the objects that had fallen out of it. He began to push them back in, but the smile faded from his face as he found himself holding Paul's statement.

A debt of two thousand pounds, this month's payment overdue, and it was in Kaye's bag. No prizes, he thought, for guessing how that had come about. He remembered the uncertainty flickering across her face when she'd spoken of her brother, as though she were trying to steel herself to ask him a favor. She'd decided against it, but then found a much neater approach.

And it was the cutest tactic that had ever been tried on him. Bored with spending money! She'd looked almost like a saint as she said it, and he'd known a wrench of tenderness in his heart. Boy, had he been fooled!

He almost gave a whistle of admiration. As a shrewd operator himself he respected an even shrewder operator. If only it wasn't this particular woman who was cheating him. She could have hurt him, if any woman could. Luckily, no woman could.

He heard Kaye returning and quickly slipped the statement into his desk.

"I don't know which of them is the greater baby!" she exclaimed, throwing her hands in the air. "Jack, please talk to Sam. He's a bad influence on Bertie."

"That ain't so!" Sam hollered. "*He's* a bad influence on *me*. I never got up to mischief before that old jackass came here. Tell her, Jack."

"That's right. Sam was a pattern of virtue," Jack agreed.

"And pigs fly!" Kaye said indignantly. "Come on, Grandpa, I'll take you to the doctor."

"I've seen a doctor," Bertie said. "Sam took me."

"There's nothing wrong with him," Sam said, "'cept he can't tell his left from his right."

"I wash my hands of the pair of you," Kaye said, exasperated and laughing at the same time.

"Does anybody mind if I have my office back?" Jack asked plaintively. "I've got a heavy day, and I'm badly in need of coffee."

"I'll make it, and we'll have it together," Kaye said eagerly.

"Thanks, but Mary's making it. Ah, there she is. Now you'll have to leave us, I'm afraid."

With a sinking heart Kaye saw that the indifferent look was there again in his eyes. His brief warmth to her might never have happened.

But it *had* happened. She was sure of it. For one moment the curtain had lifted, only to fall again, leaving her more cruelly isolated than before. She turned quickly away so that her pain might not appear in her face, and left the room.

"I wonder if Dad will be home yet," Georgy said as they drove home after an evening out watching a Disney movie.

"He did mention he had a lot of work to do," Kaye said vaguely. "Did you say something, Sam?" The old man had snorted behind her.

"Not a thing," he said.

Bertie wasn't with them. He'd declared loftily that

the entertainment wasn't sufficiently intellectual, which Kaye had translated for the other two as meaning that he'd seen it eight times already.

They arrived to find an unfamiliar van in the drive, with Hoskins Plumbers written on the side.

"Had a spot of bother with the pipes," Bertie explained when they went in.

"Can't go out and leave you, without there's trouble," Sam informed him.

"If you will live in a house that's falling to pieces," Bertie riposted.

"It wasn't falling to pieces before you arrived."

Neither Kaye nor Georgy were alarmed by this conversation, which was par for the course with those two. Bertie and Sam abused each other constantly, blackguarded each other mercilessly and loved each other dearly.

The plumber was just descending the stairs, declaring that all was now well. He announced that his bill would be along soon, and bid them a cheery goodnight.

"I'll be down to make some tea in a moment," Kaye called, mounting the stairs.

In her room she tossed her jacket onto the bed and was heading for her little bathroom when the door opened and Jack walked out, naked. The next moment she'd collided with him.

She had a close-up view of the alarm that sprang into his eyes. He grabbed her to steady himself and she had a brief, giddy sensation of being held against his bare chest. She put up her hands to his arms and let them fall again at once. After weeks with no contact this sudden collision left her senses reeling. Jack's

body was slightly damp from a shower. Kaye was
shocked by the intensity of her own reaction. She
wanted to embrace him and back away from him at
the same time. He mustn't suspect how he affected
her, but the blood was throbbing through her veins.

"I'm sorry," he said sharply. "My shower wasn't
working, so I used yours. I didn't think you'd be home
yet."

"It's all right. You don't need to apologize.
Jack—"

He backed into the bathroom without waiting for
her to finish, emerging a moment later with a towel
wrapped around his loins. That told Kaye all she
needed to know. He didn't want her to see him naked.
He just didn't want her. That was it.

Without anything being said it had simply become
accepted that Bertie was there to stay. Sam had always
regretted losing touch with his old partner in crime,
and now that they were, as he put it, "six years older
and six years sillier," he had no intention of letting it
happen again. Bertie moved his things lock, stock and
barrel into Sam's part of the house, and the two em-
barked cheerfully on their second childhoods, although, as Bertie waggishly observed, it was a moot
point whether Sam had ever left his first.

Under Sam's erratic tutelage Bertie learned to play
golf, including driving a buggy, to the danger of
everyone on the course. They passed many a happy
day in this way, winding up with riotous evenings out.
Twice they were returned home, pie-eyed, by the resigned and exasperated police.

Kaye was glad to have Bertie there, both for his

sake and her own. But she could have done without her grandfather's sharp eyes, which saw beneath the smiling mask she put on for the world.

"Of course I'm happy," she said when he first asked. "I've gotten everything I could possibly want."

"Have you, darling?" Bertie asked gently. "That's all right, then."

Sam, in his turn, asked his son what ailed him, and received much the same reply.

"Say what you like," Sam retorted stubbornly, "but there's something wrong between you two. I don't know what more you want. You've got a beautiful wife who's nuts about you—"

"Sam…" Jack began in a warning voice.

"Married little more than a month and you're not even sharing a room."

"I've spent most of that time on the injured list," Jack reminded him.

"Excuses. You don't act like a married couple."

"Sam," Jack said through gritted teeth, "you're my father. I love and respect you, and I'd do anything for you, but—"

"That I should live to hear a son of mine talk like that!" Sam exclaimed, incensed.

"What?"

"I raised you to speak out, not pussyfoot around words like you was afraid of them. If you're trying to tell me to mind my own damned business, at least have the guts to say it plain."

"Mind your own damned business!"

"That's better!"

When the two old men compared notes, there was no comfort for either of them.

''She won't tell me a thing.'' Bertie sighed. ''First time that's ever happened.''

''Same here,'' Sam said heavily. ''He actually told me to mind my own damned business. My son said that!''

He gave a melancholy sigh.

''Kaye, I'm out of money, and there's a collection today,'' Georgy said as they arrived at school one morning.

''You should have plenty of your allowance left.''

''I know I should have, but I haven't. Just a little. *Please,* Stepmother.''

''You can cut out that stepmother routine,'' Kaye said. ''All right, just a little.'' She rooted around in her bag, found her purse and gave Georgy some money. The girl thanked her and dashed out of the car.

Kaye looked into the bag to find an unfamiliar paper that her fingers had discovered. As she drew it out her eyes widened in horror.

It was Paul's credit card statement. On it was written the words ''Paid in full,'' followed by the date, in Jack's handwriting.

Kaye sat staring, feeling her heart beat strongly with something that felt almost like fear. Jack had paid Paul's debt. But how?

She snatched up the car phone. When Paul came on the line she wasted no time on preliminaries. ''Did you send that statement to Jack?'' she demanded furiously.

''Hold on—?''

''That credit card statement I wouldn't pay for you. Did you dare send it to him?''

"Of course not. I left it in your bag. I reckoned when you found it and had time to think—"

"I've only just found it, and it's been paid by Jack. I knew nothing about it. Paul, how could you do this to me?"

"Hey, what's all the fuss about? He'll never miss it."

"That's not the point," she said frantically.

"Okay, okay, I'll pay it back."

"Using what?"

"The money I'm going to be earning. I've gotten a job."

"Really?"

"It's true, I swear it."

"I'm glad. What sort of a job?"

"Selling. The basic pay isn't much, but I've got a company car, and I'll get commission."

Despite her anger, she was pleased. Paul's looks and personality would be a help to him as a salesman. He might yet manage to get his life straight.

"How did it happen?"

"I got a phone call from a man called Lionel North, who runs a clothing firm. It seems he'd heard of me from a friend of a friend."

"But what had he heard?"

"Nothing bad, so don't sound like that. Someone had told him I had potential and he said why didn't I drop in for a chat? I did and we got on fine. I start straightaway. Now then, admit you didn't think I had it in me to be a success."

She was too relieved to point out that he hadn't actually achieved success yet. The future might yet be bright.

"I'll pay Jack what I owe him, sis. Honest."

"Just see that you do."

But when she hung up, she felt very little better. This was still a disaster. She remembered now, that day in Jack's office, how she'd knocked her bag onto the floor as she rushed out to see Bertie's injuries. Jack had picked it up. He must have found the statement then, taken it and paid it without a word.

Because he thought that was what she wanted from him.

She said it over again to herself, trying to comprehend the monstrous discovery. Jack thought she was using him to fund Paul's extravagances. And he regarded it as so much a matter of course that he'd paid the debt without even mentioning it to her.

It was practically an insult.

Chapter Seven

Kaye's anger carried her through the rest of the day, working at the nursery, collecting Georgy and returning home with her. She planned to spend the evening alone. She didn't even want to speak to Jack until she'd sorted out her feelings.

But she couldn't escape entirely. Bertie had a bad case of the snuffles, and she was concerned for him. He resisted all her attempts to send him to bed, and there was a wicked glint in his eyes.

She discovered why when a taxi drew up outside the house at about seven o'clock. "Who is that for?" she asked, frowning.

"Me," Sam said, appearing in the hall, Bertie beside him. "We're going out on the town."

"Grandpa, you shouldn't be going out with your cold," Kaye protested.

"Best thing for a cold is a slug of whiskey," Sam pronounced. "I'm taking my pal out for medicinal purposes."

"But why the taxi?"

"Because we're going to get very drunk," Sam said with offended dignity. "You're not suggesting that I should *drive?*"

"Henry can take you," Jack suggested.

"And hover around me like a mother hen? No, thanks. We're going to enjoy ourselves."

"At least tell me where you're going," Kaye pleaded.

"To the Rose and Crown. They've got a new, pretty barmaid. C'mon Bertie."

They swept out, leaving Jack shaking his head and grinning ruefully. "I hope I've got his spirit when I'm that age," he said.

Kaye had already begun to walk away. "Have a drink with me?" Jack called after her.

"No, thank you, I'm busy," she said coolly.

"Doing what?"

"I'm helping out with some paperwork at the day care center."

"Is everything going all right there?"

"Splendidly, thank you."

"Kaye, have I done something to offend you?"

"Not a thing."

"I only ask because you don't usually snub me."

"That's nonsense, Jack. How could I snub you when I have every reason to be grateful to you? You're being fanciful."

"I'm not a fanciful man." He strolled over to where she'd paused at the foot of the stairs. "Too little imagination is my besetting sin, not too much. Why are you angry with me?"

He towered over her, and the impact of his close presence almost weakened her resolve to say nothing. He was her Jack who could charm her with a word or a smile, and she loved him even while she was furious with him. But she couldn't bring herself to speak. She was no match for him. He would simply shrug and imply that she was making a fuss about nothing, and she would feel more ashamed and troubled than ever.

"I've told you I'm not angry," she said with a smile that, had she known it, was as defensive as his own. "Now I must get on with my work."

She went upstairs, leaving him looking after her, puzzled.

About ten o'clock Kaye went downstairs to make herself some tea. She took some to Jack in the study. He was stretched out on the sofa, reading a financial report. He glanced up and gave her a smile that contained a question. Her coolness earlier in the evening had left him confused.

"Thanks," he said. "Going to bed?"

"Not yet. I'm going out to collect Grandpa from the Rose and Crown."

He raised an eyebrow, giving his face the mischievous look that made her heart turn over. "You think Sam can't take care of him?"

"Of course he can't. Sam's just as bad."

"True. I'll come with you."

"There's no need. I can manage."

"I said I'll come with you," he repeated firmly. "My car or yours?"

"Mine. I want to drive."

As they drove he observed that they should get there at about "chucking-out time." But they missed the ejection of Sam and Bertie by a couple of hours.

"I'm used to throwing out youngsters," observed the affronted landlord, "but at that age you expect them to behave themselves. Rosie was most upset."

"Don't you believe it," the pretty barmaid said. "They were real gentlemen, and it's always nice to be paid compliments."

"But where did they go?" Kaye asked worriedly.

"The Anchor, I think."

"It's just down the road," Jack said. "We'll pick them up there."

But when they reached The Anchor there was no sign of the two elderly reprobates. After searching the crowded pub for several minutes they approached the bar.

"Oh, them!" the barmaid said immediately. "Yes, I remember them. Knocking it back like they had hollow legs."

"But where are they?" Kaye said, urgently looking around.

"Oh, they left ages ago. Said they were going around all the pubs in the area."

"A pub crawl," Jack groaned. "That's all we need."

"They can't have gone far," said Kaye, who'd been gathering more details from one of the customers. "By the sound of it they were barely propping each other up." She turned back to the man. "Is there anything else you can tell us?"

"Only that they were singing 'Sweet Peggy O'Reilly,'" he volunteered.

"Is that bad?" Kaye asked when Jack groaned again.

"The worst. When Sam starts on 'Peggy O'Reilly' he's pretty far gone. If he sings the alternative words he can get arrested."

As they emerged into the street he was doing wild calculations. "It's nearly closing time. With any luck, wherever they went next, they'll have stayed put. The King's Head is just five minutes down there. It's worth a chance."

He seized her hand and hurried away. Kaye had to run to keep up with him. In a few moments The King's Head came into view, the sign swinging in the breeze. To their dismay the tables outside were already being cleared and people were drifting away. But a buxom barmaid, her hands filled with mugs, recognized the descriptions at once.

"They dropped in, but they didn't stay when they saw we were closing. Said they wanted a real night out and they were off to find a place that stayed open late."

"That's got to be The Shining Star," Jack said. "It's the only nightspot in staggering distance."

"Sam had no right to take him there," Kaye said crossly. "Bertie's not well."

"One little cold? With the amount of booze Sam's poured into him tonight he'll probably never have a cold again."

"It's all very well talking like that, but I don't just mean a little cold. Bertie isn't strong. You know he had a heart attack, and the way he lives he'll likely have another one. What would you and Sam understand about that? You're both so disgustingly healthy.''

''You make that sound like a crime,'' Jack objected. ''What are you pitching at me for?''

She was on edge in a way that had nothing to do with their fruitless search. Sitting beside Jack in the car, too close to him for comfort, had made her nerves jangle. Now that they were walking she would have liked to keep her distance, but he grasped her hand in his and there was no escaping his physical impact. She was furious with him. She wanted desperately to kiss him. She wanted to walk away and never see him again. She wanted to stay with him forever.

''There it is,'' he said at last. ''Let's hope they haven't been booted out of there, too.''

As nightspots went, The Shining Star was at the unsubtle end of the market, with a colorful neon sign flickering brazenly in the darkness. They were shown downstairs to where a garish floor show was in full swing. The room wasn't large, and even in the poor light they could see that there was no sign of Bertie and Sam.

''Well, that's it,'' Jack said, sitting down with a sigh of exasperation. ''I don't know what to suggest next.''

''Don't tell me that,'' Kaye said stormily. ''You can't just say you've lost my grandfather and haven't any ideas.''

''*I've* lost—? I didn't lose Bertie, he lost himself. Sam's missing, too, in case you haven't noticed.''

''That's different. Sam knows what he's doing. Grandpa's never known what he was doing in his entire life.''

''For once we're in agreement. What's that noise?''

"Your mobile's ringing," Kaye snapped.

Jack answered the phone, shouting, "Hallo?"

"Dad?"

"Georgy?"

"It's all right. They're home."

"What?"

"They got back in a taxi five minutes ago. They're just having a nightcap now."

"A nightcap?"

"To 'round the evening off,'" Georgy quoted, chuckling.

"Well, I'll be— Thanks, darling. That's a weight off my mind." He shut off the phone and looked at Kaye. "I hardly know how to tell you this, but they're home. They must have gone in one door of this place and out the other, straight into a taxi. So that's all right."

"All right?"

"Aren't you glad Bertie's safe?"

"Of course I'm glad he's safe. Now I can wring his neck."

"I feel much the same," Jack admitted. "I'm used to Sam's wild ways, but tonight he's gone too far. It's time he started acting his age." He sighed. "Oh, what the hell! Now we're here, let's stay for a while. After that chase I need something for my nerves."

"But I'm not dressed for a nightclub," she said, regarding her ordinary dress with dismay.

"Neither am I, but that didn't stop them letting us in. Now they can feed us."

The floor show was coming to an end, and they could hear themselves talk. If there was one thing Jack understood it was the art of being a perfect host. He consulted Kaye's preferences, made suggestions from the menu to please her and was never lost for the right words. His jokes were genuinely funny, and several times she laughed. But inwardly it was a different story. The resentment she'd felt toward him all day was growing.

Jack had claimed to lack imagination, but even so, he couldn't be unaware of the tension in the air. At last he sighed and fell silent, with the air of a juggler putting away the clubs.

"I get the feeling I should taste my coffee very carefully," he said to nobody in particular. "Arsenic, strychnine, cyanide—I believe they're all effective."

"Don't be absurd," she said, trying to laugh it off.

"Kaye, you've been as mad as a wasp all day. Don't deny it."

"All right, I won't."

"So? Have I let you down in some way? Am I keeping you short? Does Paul need some help?"

"That's it!" she flashed. "That's your first thought, isn't it? I'm a little out of sorts, so you assume I'm sulking because I want money."

"I'm sorry. But if it isn't money—"

"Oh, but it is. In one sense money is at the bottom of everything that's wrong with us."

"I beg your pardon?"

In silence Kaye opened her purse, took out the statement and pushed it across the table to him. "How *dare* you!" she breathed. "How dare you pay that behind my back, and not even tell me!"

He stared. "I thought you wanted me to."

"If I'd wanted you to I'd have asked you."

"You don't need to ask. We both understand that."

"I beg your pardon?"

Jack's answer was a smile. In the tolerant irony of that smile she saw everything in their relationship that made her ashamed, and her anger grew.

"You took that paper from my bag," she said furiously.

"It fell out. I did us both a favor by paying it discreetly."

"I didn't want you to pay it. Paul asked me to and I turned him down. He slipped it in my bag when I wasn't looking."

That caught his attention, she was glad to see. "You turned him down?"

"I want him to stand on his own feet. Luckily he seems to be learning to do that. He's got a job, and he says he'll pay you back every penny."

Before the words were out she knew that she'd fallen victim to another delusion. Jack's wry expression gave everything away.

"You found him that job?" she breathed.

He shrugged. "Lionel North Garments makes sports clothes. M&M is their chief customer, and I own some shares in the firm. They needed a sock rep, and it isn't a very demanding job. The socks sell themselves. Paul will only have to drive around the established outlets, refilling the shelves. I thought it would please you."

"You thought it would please me to know that my family is leeching off you? Thank you!"

"Kaye, why bother with this? We made a bargain. I'm trying to keep my side of it, even though your side might be called patchy."

"Would you mind explaining that remark?"

"You were going to marry Vane for Paul's sake. I

stopped that, so you married me instead. You even gave me the big come-on before the wedding.''

"I did what?''

"Remember how you kissed me when I came to your room that first day? I'd just given you Paul's documents. You knew he was safe and you were all over me. And that night in the garden, you started making love to me, and I began to remember things—about that time we nearly made love on Singleton, how sweet and lovely you were, how full of warmth. I thought what a lucky man I was to have found you again. Then Bertie interrupted us. I wonder how far you'd have gone if he hadn't. Far enough to make sure you kept me on the hook, or did you think backing off was a better tactic?''

"How dare—''

"But when I'd served my purpose you gave me the cold shoulder. I have to admire your nerve. Most women would have let me into their bed just once, to be on the safe side. You didn't even bother with that.''

"Do you have the nerve to suggest—?''

"I'm suggesting that you played your hand brilliantly. You've changed a lot from the girl I knew in the Caribbean. That girl was loving and giving, and I thought she always would be.'' He shrugged. "But time does change people. I have no real complaints. You're doing a great job with Georgy.''

"And that's what you hired me for, isn't it?'' she said, her eyes kindling.

"Hired? I thought we got married. That was stupid of me. Boy, have you learned a thing or two about business transactions!''

Shocked, Kaye stared at him, realizing that there

was no protest she could make. She had thrown Jack out of her bedroom on their wedding night, leaving him to think whatever he liked. Yet, irrationally, she was angry that he'd assumed the worst. She was even more angry at his cynical acceptance of what he supposed was her deviousness.

"Don't scowl at me," he said mildly. "You'll curdle the wine."

"Scowling's the least of it," Kaye said darkly. "If you knew what I'm thinking about you this minute you wouldn't sit there so easily."

"Perhaps I should duck."

"Perhaps you should. I'd like to—" She struggled for words. "I'd like to walk right out of here so that I don't have to look at you anymore tonight. And I think that's just what I'll do."

Kaye rose sharply and pushed back her chair. Before Jack had time to realize that she was serious, she was striding away from the table.

"Waiter!" he called hurriedly. By the time he'd paid the bill Kaye was far enough ahead of him to have reached the car. When he caught up she had the engine running.

"I suppose I should be glad you didn't drive off and leave me," he said, looking through the driver's window. "Move over. I'll drive."

"You will not," she seethed, staring straight ahead.

His answer was to reach in and pull the key from the ignition. "Kaye, I don't really understand any of this. I'm a plain man, lost in a maze. I've never seen you in a temper before, and it's quite a sight. But one thing I do know, and that is that you're not driving a car while you're in this state. You may not care if we get home alive, but I do.''

"Then I'll walk," she snapped. She got out and slammed the door. She was beyond being rational.

"Get back into the car," he said quietly.

"Don't tell me what to do. You get back in. Drive home. I'd rather walk.'' She turned and stormed off.

After a moment he fell into step beside her. "Fine, we'll both walk. It's not far. We've come around in a circle."

When they'd gone a little way in silence he said, "You're really good and mad at me, aren't you?"

"Ten out of ten for observation!" she snapped.

"Have I said something that offended you?"

"Calling your wife a devious schemer might be considered offensive in some circles," she said in a tight voice. "Not in yours, obviously."

"I thought I was praising your astuteness."

"If that's praise, I'd hate to be there when you insult someone."

"You're limping," he said suddenly.

"I'm not," she snapped.

"Those are new shoes. You shouldn't have worn them for walking."

It was true, but nothing would make her admit it, even though every step was painful.

"Come back and get into the car," he said, taking her arm.

"Stop telling me what to do."

"You're right," he said, moving swiftly and determinedly. "Words are wasted on you."

"Put me down at once. Did you hear me?"

"I heard you, I heard you."

"Then do it."

His only answer was to tighten his arms, holding her even more closely against his chest. "Gee, if I married a shrew! Look at it this way—you've got the advantage. You can nag me all you want, and while I'm carrying you, there isn't a thing I can do about it."

"If you think I'm just nagging, I'm wasting my time. For heaven's sake, put me down!"

"Not until you tell me the rest. Come on, there's more. Give."

"It's not my fault that we haven't—that nothing's happened between us since we married."

"Isn't it?"

"You've kept your distance. I know you were injured, but you're over that now. You've stayed well away."

"Only because you made it very clear that's what you wanted."

"That first night—after what I—" Kaye struggled to assemble her thoughts. It was hard, because being held close against Jack's chest was sending her senses into a whirl. She knew she was handling this all wrong, but the tension that had been building up in her for weeks was coming to the boil and nothing could stop it now.

"You deceived me, Jack. All that talk about reclaiming my promise—making me feel you needed me—I believed it. You had no right to do that to me."

"You did give me a promise. Anything, any time, any place. I didn't imagine that, did I?"

"But that's not why you interrupted my wedding. You just pretended."

He stared at her, and the baffled expression on his face drove her to say frantically, "I *know,* Jack. I know the truth. Grandpa blurted it out at the reception. He asked you to find a way of saving me. Can you imagine how that makes me feel? It was bad enough to know you'd only married me because you'd been backed into a corner, but at least I thought there was something you really wanted from me."

"Kaye, I can't cope with all this subtlety. You're making something complicated that's actually very simple. Okay, Bertie called and asked my help. Luckily I remembered your promise, and that gave me the idea. Are you saying this is what was bothering you on our wedding night?"

"Of course it was. I felt dreadful, like a charity case. And you kept talking about how you'd thought of me over the years. I know you meant to be kind, but it made everything worse because I knew it wasn't true, and I wanted to scream at you to stop."

"I wish you had. We could have sorted this out then."

"It can't be sorted out, don't you see? Everything about our marriage is wrong."

"Kaye, why don't you just stop talking and kiss me?"

She'd been wondering that herself for the past few minutes. Her face was unavoidably close to his, and somehow her arms had crept around his neck. It was a simple matter to tighten them and lay her mouth on his. Once it was there, no power on earth could have made her remove it. His lips felt so good, so right against hers.

His arms were occupied holding her up, so he

couldn't use them as he'd have liked to, but he made up for it by moving his mouth against hers in ways there was no mistaking. He had wide, well-shaped lips, and he used them expertly to speak without words, communicating a timeless message. She answered in kind, wreathing her fingers in his hair and giving herself up to the pleasures of kissing him.

She had no idea how long she enjoyed herself like this, but she did, finally, come out of her dream to the realization that she was still being carried.

"People will be staring at us," she murmured.

"They are."

Startled, she looked up and realized that they were no longer in the street. While she'd been entranced in his arms, Jack had reached the house and walked straight in. They were in the hallway, and Kaye had no idea how long they'd been there. Just above them, leaning over the banister, were Bertie and Sam, well-oiled and gleeful.

Still with her in his arms, Jack continued on up the stairs. "Night, Sam, night, Bertie," he said.

The blood was pounding in Kaye's veins, and she was beyond speech. But she blew a kiss to the two old men as Jack carried her past and on to her bedroom. When she'd kicked the door closed Jack stood there in the darkness, still with her in his arms.

"Mrs. Masefield," he whispered, "are you going to go on fretting about things that don't matter, or are you going to make love to your husband?"

She answered him, not in words but by touching his face with her fingertips, in a gesture of infinite tenderness. Gently he set her on her feet, putting both arms around her and kissing her deeply. Happiness flooded her, and all the cares and anxieties that had kept them apart fell away.

"Are you sure this time?" he asked softly.

"Oh, yes," she breathed. "Quite sure. I've been sure since—since our wedding night." Even now, the truth couldn't be told. But perhaps she was getting closer.

"I wish I'd known," he murmured, kissing her again. "I'd looked forward to you, thought about you...."

"What kind of thoughts?" she asked, for the pleasure of hearing the answer.

His ready laughter came surging up even through the growing intensity of his lovemaking. "Very basic, very disrespectful—not gentlemanly at all..." He was undressing her as he spoke, opening her buttons, expertly slipping garments from her until the last one had gone.

"I don't want you to be respectful," she said. "Not just now."

"Why don't you show me what you want?"

It was too good an invitation to pass up. This was the third time she'd been here, and nothing was going to be allowed to snatch it away again. She was naked, and it was intolerable that he should still be fully dressed.

But she had only to make the first movements. When he felt her fingers at his buttons and knew that this time she was here to stay, Jack moved swiftly to complete the job.

Once before, she'd seen him naked, the day she'd found him leaving her bathroom. It had ended badly, but the vision of masculine beauty had stayed with her, burned into her brain. Now he was everything she remembered, with one marvelous difference. He was hers.

He drew her down onto the bed and pushed her gently back against the pillows. ''Let me look at you for a while,'' he murmured. ''There's no hurry.''

He was eager for her, but his finely tuned physical instincts told him that she wasn't quite ready. He wanted to make everything right. She was special, enchanting.

She lay there, shy but proud that the sight of her pleased him. Her breath was coming in quick gasps as desire mounted in her, and she felt as though her urgency must be revealed by her whole body. Her breasts were heavy, the nipples proudly peaked, surrounded by soft brown aureoles.

No other man had ever excited her. Their kisses had left her flesh chill and unresponsive. But with Jack everything in her seemed to riot out of control at once. How could she ever have pushed him away, when she craved him so much?

He gathered her in his arms, holding her closely against his big body, touching her gently. A delicate perfume arose from between her breasts, making his senses reel, and he laid his mouth over hers, slipping his tongue between her lips and beginning a flickering exploration.

Kaye closed her eyes and gave herself up to the best and sweetest experience of her life. She'd thought she desired Jack, but that desire was a tiny match flame beside the fire that was being ignited inside her by the devastating movements of his tongue. Returning a kiss like that was one easy lesson, and she gave back passion for passion.

She felt the light touch of his fingers on her inner thighs. She'd waited so long for her moment, and now it had come. When he slipped between her legs there was a momentary sense of the unfamiliar. But this was her Jack, whom she loved and trusted. His eyes smiled into hers, asking if all was well, and she smiled back, slipping her arms confidently about his neck.

Then he was inside her, moving slowly until she was used to the feel of him. But she was easy with him almost at once, falling naturally into his rhythm, gasping out her delight.

It had startled Jack to find her still a virgin, but now he was glad he'd gone carefully. He held back, wanting her first experience to be perfect, but even so his own desire was overwhelming him. He'd spent the past few weeks frustratedly imagining this moment, and now his movements became infused with urgency despite himself.

Kaye felt as though flames were raging along every nerve, burning her up in the ecstasy of the union she'd longed for. As his thrusts became deeper she arched against him, crying out with longing and fulfillment, until his voice mingled with hers in a long sigh of pleasure.

Tears stung her eyes as he left her, but his arms still held her strongly, offering tenderness as passion faded. It was a wordless tenderness, for everything had already been said. She'd come home at last, and never more so than when she fell asleep in his arms.

She awoke to find herself still held against him. In the gray light of dawn she could see his eyes on her, full of their shared knowledge. ''Good morning, wife,'' he said softly.

''Good morning, husband.''

The words had a second meaning. They were greeting each other like people who'd only just met, as, in a sense, they had; asking questions about how things had changed between them.

''You were everything I hoped you'd be,'' he said. With a teasing light in his eye he added, ''At last.''

''Must we—must we talk about that?'' she asked, speaking with difficulty because already her desire was rising again.

''I don't want to talk about anything right now,'' he agreed, laying his lips over hers. ''I want something very different. And I always get what I want.''

Already she knew him as if they'd shared not one but a hundred lovings, and she was ahead of him now, so that he laughed at her eagerness.

''Not so fast,'' he said tenderly. ''We've got time.''

''We've got lost time to make up,'' she insisted. ''Now, *you* come here.''

''Yes, *ma'am!*''

It was the same but better, more beautiful, more exciting, but slower, with time to savor each sensation to the full. As Jack thrust deeply into her she drove back against him, welcoming him with every movement.

He felt that silent welcome and his heart rejoiced, for right until the last minute he'd half expected her to change her mind and lead him on another mystery tour through the workings of her mind. But she was all his now, her arms about his neck, her slight body fitting against his powerful one as though they'd been made for each other. Even in that short time she'd grown in confidence and knowledge, so that she could let him know what pleased her, and he could respond with delight.

"How could you be so foolish?" he asked when the tumult had died down. "What does it matter how we met again?"

"I don't know," she murmured against him. "It seemed so important at the time."

In the clear light of day she could see that Jack had been right. None of the things that had seemed so important before mattered in the slightest. Nothing mattered except the ecstatic fulfillment she'd found in his arms, and the feeling of being his woman, and his alone.

"I didn't like all the giving to be on your side," she tried to explain.

"You can't really believe that now you've met Elsie. You see how big my problems are."

"But you never thought of coming to me until Bertie asked you to help me."

He grinned. "Of course. Do you really think I could kidnap a bride from her wedding unless I knew it was what she wanted? I may be shameless, but I'm not *that* shameless."

She joined in his laughter, and the moment passed.

Jack began tracing a finger along the outline of her waist, her hip, her thigh.

"I never truly thought you'd still be a virgin," he mused softly. "But I'm glad. You were always different from other women, and you still are. I like that."

"Other women?" she ventured to ask. "You mean Jenny and Sally and Dora and Heather and—"

"Hey, enough of that," he said hastily, laying his finger over her lips. "Those days are past. I'm a respectable old married man now."

"Respectable?" she echoed hilariously. "You?"

"A reformed character, I swear it."

"Don't reform too much," she begged. "You wouldn't be so much fun."

"That's one thing I remember from Singleton. You understood me perfectly, even in those days. Still do, huh?"

"It's my speciality," she assured him. "But I'm the only one, aren't I?"

"I beg your pardon?"

"You don't understand me at all. Or you couldn't have thought what you did. Get your ring on my finger and chuck you out of my bed, indeed!"

"But that's what you did." He defended himself. "How could I work out the truth? I didn't know what Bertie had told you. And I'm not good at how women's minds work at the best of times." An aggrieved note entered his voice. "You all seem to live on another planet, and I'm lost because someone's swung all the signposts around."

"Why, you chauvinist!" she said indignantly. "Straight out of the Ark. Men don't talk like that anymore."

"Oh, yes, they do, my sweet. Most of them are cautious enough not to let women hear them, but me— I never had any caution."

She sat up in bed, a shameless naked nymph. He

lay back, his arms behind his head, surveying her with pleasure.

"Let's stay here all day," he said, and, laughing, she threw herself into his arms.

"Don't you have to go to work?"

"The hell with work!"

Chapter Eight

Keeping up with Georgia took all Kaye's ingenuity. Like any normal teenager, the girl blew hot and cold as her moods changed. She was as easygoing as her father and would happily chatter with Kaye, but she also had her mother's temper, and any hint of restriction roused it.

"I can see why she doesn't want to be treated like a child," Kaye said to Jack one evening when they were eating alone. Georgia was spending the evening at the home of one of her classmates, and the two old men had joined some of Sam's friends for a night's carousing. "She's too self-possessed and sophisticated for her years."

"What's she done now?" Jack asked with a grin.

"Only bought me another expensive dress." Kaye sighed.

"Fine."

"But we were supposed to be shopping for her. She simply took control and turned it into a buying spree for me. She kept waving her hand and saying loftily, 'My mom would like to see something else.'"

"Mom? That's good."

"Don't be fooled. She calls me that when she's sweet-talking me. When I said she had to be home by ten tonight I became the wicked witch again."

"I know. She appealed to me to overrule you."

"I hope you didn't."

"I'm afraid I did."

"Jack, the only way to survive Georgy is for us to present a united front."

"Actually I said she could stay overnight with her friend. I thought it would give us a little time together." He added slyly, "But I think your idea about a 'united front' is splendid."

"Oh, I see."

He grinned. "I thought you would. Are you going to be long eating that?"

"It's funny, but I've lost my appetite."

"Come on." He held out his hand and she took it, following him eagerly upstairs.

There they tumbled each other in bed, vigorously, laughing like teenagers. A moment to recover their breath and they were ready for the fray again, this time with a little subtlety now that the first frantic urgency was gone.

Then Kaye bounced out of bed, threw on a robe and collected their supper from downstairs. After a bite to eat and a bottle of wine they were fully rested, this time making love slowly and with tenderness before sleeping in each other's arms.

This was their life now. Any conversation could be turned into a declaration of passion. Their ecstatic physical harmony colored the world, giving a new meaning to every word and gesture, no matter how trivial.

In that blissful atmosphere it was tempting to forget about Elsie, but Jack's ex-wife still had some tricks up her sleeve. One afternoon, when Kaye and Georgia were having tea in a restaurant, the woman herself walked in. They were in the middle of an argument, and it was the worst possible time for Georgy's mother to appear out of the blue.

"Mom!" Georgy sounded surprised but not overwhelmed with joy.

"My baby!" Elsie cried, flinging her arms about her daughter. "Did you think your mommy had forgotten you?"

Georgy didn't answer this, but her eyes had a slightly hunted look as she disentangled herself from her mother. She had a normal teenager's horror of emotional displays by adults, and Elsie was going right over the top.

Elsie plumped herself into a chair and met Kaye's eyes defiantly across the table. "Didn't know I was following you, did you? I've got friends. They've told me every move you've made."

"There was no need for that," Kaye said, more calmly than she felt. "Of course you should stay in touch with Georgy. Jack never meant to separate you completely."

"That's what you think! I don't trust him, and if

you had any sense you wouldn't, either. Don't suppose you care for anything as long as you get his money.''

''Mom, lay off Kaye,'' Georgy said awkwardly. ''It's not her fault.''

''I know just whose fault it is, my darling. Never mind. It's all over now. You're coming away with me, right this minute.''

''I can't allow that,'' Kaye said, feeling a rising tide of alarm.

''You can't stop me,'' Elsie said.

Kaye had a nightmare vision of how Jack would look at her if she let this happen. But Georgy was looking askance at her mother. ''I don't think so, Mom,'' she said awkwardly. ''I'm not ready for a trip.''

''Darling, I'll buy you all the things you want—''

''Please, not now,'' Georgy said tensely.

Quietly Kaye summoned the waiter and paid the bill. Elsie went on arguing, while Georgy's mouth had a mulish look. When Kaye said, ''We're going,'' the girl rose at once.

''You needn't think this is the end.'' Elsie spat the words at Kaye. ''You're not going to turn my baby against me.''

''You're doing that very efficiently yourself,'' Kaye told her angrily. ''Come along, Georgy.''

The girl followed her without a word, and sat in silence all the way home.

''I shouldn't have been so careless,'' Kaye said to Jack that evening. ''But I had no idea Elsie was following us.''

''Nor had I.'' He brooded. ''I'd better set someone

to keep an eye on her if she's going to do this kind of thing. Don't blame yourself.''

"But I do. If Georgy had wanted to go with her, I'm not sure I could have stopped her.''

"Luckily she didn't. Don't you see how important it is that she made her own decision to stay?''

"Elsie blew it by embarrassing Georgy in front of the whole restaurant.''

"Maybe she's beginning to see through her. And I think it's your doing.''

After that Kaye was on edge waiting for Elsie's next trick, but it didn't come. The firm Jack had hired to watch her reported that she'd departed for Monte Carlo very suddenly.

"François,'' Sam said when he heard this. "My guess is, he's run out of money and decided making up with Elsie is better than working for a living.''

"As long as it gets her out of my hair,'' Jack grunted. "Now perhaps we can have some peace.''

"There'll never be peace while that woman's on the prowl,'' Sam declared dramatically.

"She could mastermind a snatch from abroad,'' Bertie agreed.

"What are you two—?''

"Georgy will need dedicated protectors,'' Sam proclaimed in a noble voice.

"And we're ready for the challenge,'' Bertie hollered.

"Oh, God!'' Jack dropped his head in his hands.

The two old men took a fiendish delight in their self-appointed job. A trip to a safari park that Kaye had planned for herself and Georgy became a merry foursome.

"Are they supposed to be protecting *us?*" Georgy demanded when a ranger had reproved Sam for the third time for putting his head out of the car. "We'll end up having to get them out of jail."

"I know," Kaye said with a chuckle. "But it keeps them happy."

To her great pleasure her relationship with Georgy was becoming relaxed and confiding again. The four of them had a great day out and returned home singing loudly and tunelessly.

"Where did that monstrosity come from?" Sam demanded as they turned the bend in the drive. He pointed at a strange car parked outside the front door. It was a low-slung vehicle in pearl blue, lavishly adorned with chrome. A man and a woman were just getting out.

"Oh, no!" Kaye groaned. Bertie groaned even more loudly.

"It's that dreadful woman!" he exploded. "Sorry, Kaye. I know she's your mother. Ye gods! Paul's there, too."

Rhoda and Paul were just approaching the front door, but at the sound of the car they turned and waited. Rhoda fitted her face into a smile of unbearable graciousness that didn't even waver when Bertie demanded, "What are you doing here?"

"Dear Bertie, so lovely to see you again!" she gushed.

"Well, it ain't lovely to see you again," he growled.

"Just because I came to visit my daughter as any loving mother would do," Rhoda said, offended.

Kaye gave Paul a hug, glad to notice that he was looking well.

"We thought we'd pay you a little call to show you how well I'm doing now. How do you like the car? Flash, eh?"

Flash was the right word, Kaye reflected, looking out of the window. The car was sleekly ostentatious, the vehicle of a very young man who wanted to be noticed.

"Where does it come from?" she asked.

"It's mine. At least, it goes with my job. They let me choose the one I wanted."

"And you picked that one?" Kaye said, trying not to smile.

"It says something about me," Paul declared unnecessarily.

"It does that, all right!" Bertie snorted.

"Hallo, Grandpa, I didn't see you there," Paul said. He was always slightly uneasy with Bertie, knowing that his charm entirely failed on the old man.

"I'm surprised you can see anything next to that miracle of engineering," Bertie said with awful sarcasm. "It blots out the sun."

Paul's smile wavered. He had a suspicion Bertie was making fun of him, but he wasn't sure. Paul was sharp, but neither intelligent nor subtle.

"I'm glad things are working out for you," Kaye said. "The job's going well?"

"Like a dream. Here." He took an envelope from his pocket. "This is for you," he said.

She opened it and found a check for the exact amount of the credit card statement that Jack had paid.

"You see?" Paul said triumphantly. "I pay my debts. Now what do you say?"

"Paul," she said helplessly, "this check is drawn on another credit card."

"So, I'll pay it off later. The important thing is that you've got the money back."

She supposed there was something in that. At least Paul had taken the debt back onto himself, and perhaps he could repay it out of his earnings.

"Hallo—anybody there?"

Jack appeared through the front door, glancing around at his unexpected guests with only a faint look of surprise. He was given the full impact of Rhoda at her most gracious.

"You won't mind us dropping in without warning," she gushed. "I was so worried about leaving Bertie here in a state of collapse."

Kaye was ready to sink through the floor, but Jack greeted his new relatives with calm good humor and only the slightest hint of irony, which completely passed Rhoda by.

"What's that thing outside?" he asked Kaye in a low voice when the greetings were over.

"Paul's company car, apparently."

"Good grief! He's supposed to be selling socks." Jack gave a resigned sigh. "I told them to let him pick his own. I should have known better. You haven't told him that I fixed the job for him, have you?"

"Not a word."

"Good. I want him to feel self-confident, and that'll be easier if he doesn't—" He broke off as Paul approached them, all smiles.

"I've got a job now," he declared. "A good one, too."

"I'm very pleased," Jack said, straight-faced.

"I didn't have to apply for it, either. They head-hunted me. I said I couldn't consider the job unless the conditions were right. If a man doesn't set a high price on himself, nobody else is going to, right?"

"Right," Jack said blandly.

If only her brother would shut up, Kaye thought in an agony of embarrassment, or at least show a little modesty. But he burbled on, boasting of his high position and his importance to the firm. Nobody listening to him would have known he was a sock salesman.

"I can't stand this," she muttered when Paul had mercifully taken himself off. "Let me tell him the truth."

"Better not," Jack said.

"How do you think I feel when he makes a fool of himself like that?"

"Ignore it. Life's too short to worry. He'll grow up soon, and then you can really be proud of him. Do you see me losing sleep?"

"I don't think you lose sleep about anything."

"Oh, I lose sleep over one thing—quite a lot, recently."

They exchanged smiles, and at once her worries were forgotten. As long as Jack could take her into the wonderful, secret world they shared, nothing could trouble her very much.

It was a hot day and they had supper beside the swimming pool. Georgy appeared in a bikini and slipped into the water. Paul promptly stripped down to a pair of brightly colored shorts and joined her.

Jack regarded them benignly while conversing with Rhoda. Kaye wished she could hear what they were saying, but it was all a mumble until Rhoda said loudly, "Why, Jack, how nice of you! I'm sure there's no need for you to invite us if you don't want us. Of course, it would mean the world to me to be able to look after Bertie—"

"You keep clear of me," Bertie said hastily, edging away from her.

By now Kaye was beyond being embarrassed by her family. She just gave Jack a helpless look, and after a while he came and sat down beside her. "I'm doing this for my own reasons," he said. "Paul can be very useful to me right now."

"Oh, sure, I'll bet he's doubled the sock sales," she said wryly.

"Actually, they tell me he's not a bad salesman. His looks and personality work for him. But I meant something else. Watch him with Georgy."

The two young people were chasing each other around the pool. As Kaye watched, Paul lifted her high in his arms and tossed her into the water, dived after her, seized her from below and tossed her up again. Georgy was shrieking with laughter.

"I like to see her frolicking like a little kid," Jack said. "It makes me feel a little less guilty about the bit I missed."

"But she's not a little kid," Kaye warned. "I'm afraid she's getting a crush on Paul. I know it's ridiculous at her age, but she doesn't think so."

"I'd rather have her with a crush on Paul than Henri," Jack said. "When I went upstairs to get changed I got a nasty shock. I heard Georgy on the phone, talking French. My French isn't brilliant. I can do deals in it and that's all, but even I understand *mon amour*."

"Oh, no! Henri?"

"I'm sure of it, and I don't like it. Now do you see why Paul's a godsend? I know his weaknesses, but he's basically harmless. Henri is a very nasty character indeed, with some unpleasant criminal connections. Paul's taking Georgy's mind off him. And while they're both here under my eye I'm not too worried."

Kaye had to admit he was right when she saw Georgy flirting madly with Paul, but flirting with the innocence of a child playing games.

"You must watch your step," she warned her brother as they went upstairs that night. He was carrying a valise that he'd taken from the car, as was Rhoda. It was clear that they'd come with the idea of being invited to stay.

"About what?"

"About Georgy. Jack lets her make eyes at you because he'd rather you than Henri. But he's very protective about his little girl."

"Kaye, darling, your husband doesn't scare me. I'm my own man since I got this job."

Kaye was silenced.

The next day she took her mother on a shopping trip. They went to Dorrell's, where she treated Rhoda to a new outfit. As she was paying, the assistant said, "I've got a parcel here for Miss Masefield. I was about to send it...."

"I'll take it with me," Kaye said, smiling.

They went upstairs to the store's restaurant. Rhoda's manner was curious. She was proud that her daughter had "done well for herself," but she was also obscurely resentful that it was the despised child who'd exceeded her wildest expectations. She accepted the gifts that Kaye bought her, with the words, "I suppose you can afford this sort of thing all the time now."

"As long as you like them," Kaye said determinedly. "If you want to change anything—"

"Oh, no, it's fine. It'll go with the coat Paul bought me from his first week's wages. Of course, he hasn't got a lot of money to splash out like you have. He has to really work for his, but that makes it mean more that he spent it on me."

"That was very nice of him," Kaye said. She was finally facing the fact that Rhoda actively disliked her. She would make use of her, especially to advance Paul's interests. She would get what she could out of her. But she disliked her.

She tried not to feel hurt. She had Jack now, and her life with him was sweeter to her than anything else on earth. But even he didn't love her.

She left the parcel on Georgy's bed to await the moment when Harry brought her home from her last day at school before the summer vacation. The box was large and fancy, and Kaye was intrigued to know about Georgy's latest purchase.

Just as she started on supper the kitchen phone rang. It was Georgy, calling from the car. "Kaye, if Paul's there, keep him out of sight," she pleaded. "I'll die of shame if he sees me in uniform."

"Don't worry, he's not back yet," Kaye said with a chuckle.

Georgy arrived ten minutes later. Kaye met her on the steps, saying, "No sign of him. You're safe."

"Thank goodness," Georgy muttered, and fled furtively up the stairs.

It was a long, complicated meal to prepare, and by the time it was ready Jack was home, but not Paul.

"There shouldn't be anything to keep him late on a Friday," Jack mused. "Will the food spoil if we eat late?"

"It certainly will. We'll eat now. Paul can starve," Kaye said firmly.

"That's my girl! All heart."

She laughed and went up the stairs to let Georgy know the meal was ready. On the threshold of the girl's room she stopped, aghast.

"What is that you're wearing?"

Georgy swung around from the full-length mirror where she'd been surveying herself. She was wearing a long, tight-fitting dress in crimson satin. It was cut low in the front, slit up the side, and would have been daring on a woman twice her age. With her hair piled high on her head Georgy looked nothing like a schoolgirl.

"If I'd known what was in that box, nothing would have made me bring it home," Kaye declared. "Georgy, are you out of your mind? What would your father say if he saw that?"

"I suppose you're going to be a spoilsport and tell him." Georgy pouted.

"There won't be anything to tell, because it's going back."

"It's not fair. You want to keep me looking like a kid forever."

"Don't be absurd. You're growing up fast, but enjoy your youth while you have it. Come on, take it off.''

''No, you can't make me.''

Unwisely, Kaye decided to tackle this head-on. Muttering, ''Oh, yes, I can,'' she reached for Georgy and tried to get to the zip at the back. The girl twisted away violently, and there was a struggle and an ugly tearing sound.

Together they surveyed the slit at the side, longer now that the material had ripped. ''The shop won't take it back now,'' Georgy said, sounding pleased.

''No, they won't, but you're not having it, either. Take it off right now.''

Georgy shrugged and gave up the fight. Kaye packed the dress away in the box and carried it to the door. ''I'm confiscating this,'' she said.

''It's not fair,'' Georgy yelled. The ''woman'' of a moment ago was gone, replaced by a little girl in a tantrum. ''That's stealing.''

''Very well,'' Kaye said quietly. ''Complain to your father. If he tells me to give it back to you, I will.''

Checkmated, Georgy stared at her with loathing. ''You don't care if I'm miserable,'' she choked. ''You just want to ruin my life.''

''Sure I do,'' Kaye agreed affably. ''But right now I'm too busy serving supper. Let's eat first, and I'll ruin your life later.''

She went out, closing the door behind her. To her relief she could hear Paul's voice downstairs. She hurriedly hid the box in her own room and went down. ''I was about to send out a search party,'' she told her brother.

"Had a spot of car trouble, so I came home in a taxi," he said airily.

"You don't mean to say that magnificent machine let you down?" Sam asked incredulously.

"Kind of thought it might," Bertie declared to nobody in particular.

Paul scowled and followed Kaye into the kitchen. She handed him a sherry. "Can you do your job without a car?" she asked, choosing her words carefully so as not to betray how much she knew about his work.

"Well, they gave me another vehicle," Paul admitted.

"Then why not drive it home?"

"Because I wouldn't be seen dead in it by anyone who knows me," he said with a shudder. "It's a van, with company stickers all over it."

She couldn't help laughing at his horrified tone, which made him sound so much like Georgy. They were nothing but two innocent children, after all. The thought cheered her so much that she was able to greet Georgy, when she came down wearing a simple sweater and slacks, with good humor.

But her affability wasn't returned. The girl gave her a hostile glare that warned her the matter wasn't over yet.

Whatever was wrong with Paul's shiny car couldn't be put right quickly. Days passed and still he was using the van and coming home by taxi. Once he borrowed Kaye's car to take Georgy to the pictures. She agreed on condition he had the girl home by ten o'clock. To her surprise they were back before then. She began to relax.

She devoted her days to entertaining Rhoda. Under the influence of comfortable living her mother was softening, and talking to her in a comparatively friendly voice. But this gave Kaye little pleasure, since Rhoda spoke as though Kaye shared her own materialistic view of her marriage, and this grated on her.

Once when they'd just returned home after a hectic day and were sitting with long, cold drinks in the room overlooking the garden, Rhoda observed, ''Well, you've really landed on your feet, and no mistake. You knew what you were doing when you dumped Lewis, didn't you?''

''Mom, it wasn't like that.''

''Looks like it to me. Smart bit of work. But you've got to make the best of it. How long do you think your luck is going to last?''

''I don't know what you mean.''

''How long before he tires of you? You'll need a good lawyer to get you a decent settlement, but in the meantime get what you can out of him. There are a thousand ways to make a man sit up and beg.''

''Mom! Shush, please!'' Kaye whispered, turning burning eyes on Rhoda.

''I'll bet he's got a damned sight more loot than Lewis.''

''Stop it,'' Kaye choked.

''No need to act coy. I'm your mother. You've done well, but I can tell you how to do even better.''

''Did it ever occur to you that I married Jack because I loved him?'' Kaye asked in an urgent undervoice.

Rhoda gave a laugh that was almost a cackle. ''Not

for a moment, sweetie, but if that's what you're letting him think, good for you.''

"It's the truth. I've loved him for years, ever since we met on Singleton.''

"That's a good line. Did he fall for it?''

"I haven't told him,'' she said desperately.

"For Pete's sake, why not?''

"Because it would embarrass him. He's not in love with me.''

Rhoda hooted with ribald laughter. "If ever a man had the hots for a woman, he's got them for you. He can't look at you without undressing you. I've seen it.''

Kaye felt sick at hearing the beautiful desire between herself and Jack described in such a way. But before she could protest, Rhoda went on, "All right, let it go. I don't understand your game, but as long as it delivers the goods, what the hell!''

Kaye couldn't stand it a moment longer. She rose and ran out of the French doors into the garden. She needed to breathe cool, fresh air, away from the pollution of her mother's thoughts.

Somebody else also felt polluted by Rhoda's brutal greed. Jack, just arrived home and coming in search of Kaye, had heard a shrill, ugly voice as he crossed the hall.

"There are a thousand ways to make a man sit up and beg.''

He'd frozen to the spot, sick with disgust. Before he could react he heard Kaye murmur a reply. He couldn't make out the words, but he heard Rhoda's reply. *"I'll bet he's got a damned sight more loot than Lewis.''*

He strained to hear Kaye, but she was speaking too softly to hear. It didn't matter, he assured himself. He knew his Kaye. She would be rebutting her mother's vulgar suspicions. He would hear that in Rhoda's next words.

Her ugly laugh seemed to go through him. But worse still was her ominous remark, *"Not for a moment, sweetie, but if that's what you're letting him think, good for you."*

Jack went cold. What could Kaye possibly have said to produce such a response? He held himself very still, desperate to hear her voice, but Kaye's words were all delivered in an indecipherable murmur.

Then Rhoda again. *"If ever a man had the hots for a woman, he's got them for you...I don't understand your game, but as long as it delivers the goods, what the hell!"*

Silence in the hall. Jack stood as though turned to stone. Rhoda, up to her bullying tricks again. That was how he read it. Kaye would have replied as best she could, but he knew she found it hard to stand up to her mother. In a minute he would go and find her, and she would reassure him.

Somehow the word *reassure* troubled him. It suggested that he minded, and he'd spent too much of his life not minding about anything to change easily now. And why change? He had a good life with Kaye. When he told her about this they would laugh together.

It was very quiet standing there in the hall, and he could hear the air singing about his ears. After a while he walked out of the house and drove away again. Nobody saw him arrive or leave.

Chapter Nine

A man could always find urgent work if he was determined to do so, and for the first hour after returning to his office Jack worked on matters that he convinced himself couldn't wait.

But he was devoting only the upper part of his mind to them. Underneath he was in turmoil.

It was absurd to heed anything Rhoda said, especially as he hadn't heard Kaye's reply. He was happy with his wife. She gave him all he asked from her. She ran his home, protected his daughter and delighted him in bed. He resisted the thought that beyond these things he deliberately didn't ask for very much. It was his habit to expect little from anyone, especially from women. Life had taught him that a certain level of tolerant mistrust made things easier. You didn't get hurt.

It disturbed him to discover that his feelings for Kaye wouldn't fit into this neat pattern, especially as her own feelings remained a mystery. When he was with her he sometimes found himself not knowing what to say. For a man whose ability to talk fast had helped him build an empire, that was alarming.

He blinked and tried to clear his head. The screen was beginning to swim before his eyes, and there was really no more he could do tonight. But he knew that he was actually trying to put off the moment when he must decide what to do next.

The confusion of his thoughts was cut into by the shrill of the phone. It was Kaye. "It's so late I wondered when you'd be home," she said, adding with a faint chuckle, "stranger."

As soon as he heard her voice he felt all right again. This was his Kaye, whom he trusted, and all his worries seemed ridiculous. He'd prepared a speech about being unable to get home that night, but it died on his lips.

"I'll be there in half an hour," he said.

"I'll look forward to it."

He left his office at a run.

After setting down the phone Kaye sat staring into space for a while, a prey to thoughts that were apprehensive, exhilarated and excited. The scene with Rhoda earlier that day had left her in a strange mood. She'd fled, disgusted by the vulgarity of her mother's thoughts, but when she was alone, some of Rhoda's words came back to her with a new resonance.

If ever a man had the hots for a woman, he's got

them for you. He can't look at you without undressing you.

Strip away the coarseness of expression, and it meant that Jack wanted her. It might only be in one limited way, but she could use his desire—not, as Rhoda suggested, to make money from him, but to win his love.

She longed for him to come home now so that she could look at him through the new filter that had been held before her eyes. Half an hour stretched endlessly ahead. All about her the house was getting ready for bed.

Bed. She tried not to think of it. It would be a while before she could get Jack into bed and lovingly try out her newly discovered power. Bed. It would be her kingdom. Already she could feel the soft, urgent throbbing in her veins at the thought of how triumphantly she would reign there, and how glad she would make her lover.

At last she saw the lights of his car between the trees. Eagerly she began to run toward him.

Jack, traveling as fast as he dared in the drive, saw her in his headlamps at the last moment and braked sharply, cursing.

"Kaye, what the devil are you doing?" he shouted in fear.

"Sorry," she said, sliding in beside him. "I got impatient waiting for you."

"And throwing yourself under my wheels was your way of showing me?" he demanded. "You gave me the fright of my life."

For answer she hooked an arm around his neck and pulled him forward until she could clasp her mouth to his. Jack's head spun with a kiss such as he'd never known from her before.

"Kaye?"

"What's the matter? It's not the first time I've kissed you."

"It's the first time you've done it like that in a car in the middle of the drive," he pointed out in a ragged voice.

"So, there's a first time for everything."

"For Pete's sake! I've got to control this car the rest of the way."

She immediately sat back in her seat, her hands clasped demurely before her, the picture of innocence. It didn't make him feel any safer. He simply grew puzzled, trying to work out this new mood, and nearly steered the car into the grass verge.

Supper for two was laid out on the scrubbed pine table in the kitchen—his favorite cheese soufflé and a bottle of rough red wine, just as he liked it. Kaye had learned his favorite recipes from Sam, who enjoyed cooking, and executed them superbly. The two of them had a friendly rivalry going.

"Why are you looking at me like that?" Jack asked as she was serving him a second helping.

"I'm just thinking what I'm going to do to you as soon as we get upstairs," she said, meeting his gaze steadily.

He felt as if he'd been punched in the stomach, yet softly, as if with a powder puff. But he recovered his poise enough to answer teasingly, "I thought I'd go straight to sleep tonight."

"No," Kaye said simply.

"No?"

"I have other ideas."

He was enjoying the game. "Suppose I don't fall in with your ideas."

"You will," she assured him with a little smile. "You won't have any choice."

The powder puff punched him again, straight in the groin, sending waves of heated expectancy flowing through him, depriving him of his breath, his voice. She'd never spoken to him like that before, and he liked it. He loved it.

"Finish your supper," she told him.

"I'm not hungry anymore—not for food."

He wanted to strip her there and then, the way she was so clearly enticing him to do. But she shook her head.

"That's a pity, when I've made you such a nice meal," she said with a sigh. "I'd better go away while you finish."

"Hey!"

"I'm going up to have a shower. I'll be a while. I don't like to hurry."

Her sheer effrontery staggered and delighted him. Through the reeling of his senses he was vaguely aware that there was something bothering him about this situation, but his mind wasn't clear enough to sort it out now. While he was trying to pull himself together, Kaye slipped away.

She was laughing to herself with secret delight. It was working. She was going to give Jack the night of his life, but on her own terms. And he was going to enjoy every moment.

As she'd hoped and expected, Jack appeared in her bathroom barely five minutes later. She was already in the shower, standing beneath the jet of hot water. She'd been about to soap herself, but the sight of him standing on the other side of the misty glass made her set the soap down and begin to turn this way and that beneath the water. She could sense his stillness as he watched her, and knew she had his total, undivided attention. Her new, flowering confidence told her that right now the phone could have rung, the doorbell screamed and the house caught fire without distracting his attention from her one little bit.

When he finally managed to move, it was like a sleepwalker, slowly undoing the buttons of his shirt, his eyes still fixed on her through the glass. His shirt went, then his pants. Then the shower door opened.

"Thought I'd join you," he said, slipping in naked beside her and closing the door.

"I said, finish your supper first," she teased.

He grinned. "Your mouth told me to finish supper. The rest of you told me something very different."

"Think you can read me, huh?"

"Ma'am, the message you were giving out, there was no mistaking."

Looking down, she could see how well he'd understood her. He was big and powerful, throbbing with urgency, promising everything. She thought he would take her there and then, but if she could play games, so could he, and his control was wonderful. He put some soap on his hands and gently laid them on her, drawing them down from her shoulders until he could encompass her breasts in his palms. They were heavy now, the nipples already peaked with desire, and they filled his big hands.

He regarded them lovingly, brushing his thumbs

lightly back and forth against the nipples. Those tantalizingly slow movements almost sent her out of her mind, and a long sigh broke from her. She let her head fall back, offering herself up to him without defense.

"Mrs. Masefield, you're a liar."

"What?"

"You let me think you were all cool and indifferent, and that was the biggest lie you ever told."

"Could be," she murmured. "I'm still considering the matter."

"Let me help you," he said huskily.

The sudsy water laced down her, making her body slippery, so that his hands glided easily over her contours, in and out, over curves and valleys, until they came to rest on her behind, cupping it in both hands. He bent his head so that he could inflict soft, tormenting kisses on the delicate skin beneath her ears, the way he knew she liked. He knew every inch of her by now, what pleased her a little, a lot, what could drive her into a frenzy. Yet tonight he was discovering that he barely knew her at all. And it thrilled him.

He rinsed her down, washing away the last of the soap, leaving her as damp and fresh as a water nymph. Kaye had fast become an expert in the caresses he liked, and also the ones that reduced him to helpless delight. So she ran her fingertips friskily up his chest and down again, making every tiny movement tell.

"What—are you doing?" he asked raggedly.

"Only trying to please you," she said. "Doesn't that please you?"

"You—know it does."

"Yes," she murmured, her lips against his chest, "I know it does. And I know what else pleases you."

"I guess you do," he said slowly. "What now?" He'd never asked that question of any woman before, but he desperately wanted to know what this woman's answer would be.

She considered, her head charmingly on one side. "I—haven't quite decided. What would you say to simply getting a good night's sleep?"

"What I'd say to that isn't fit for a lady's ears," he said raggedly.

She actually had the nerve to laugh, regarding him with impish delight. "Oh, Jack," she teased. "Oh, Jack!"

"Why, you cheeky little urchin!" He grated the words out before his mouth descended forcefully on hers.

She was still laughing at him. He could feel it right through the kiss, through her own response and his. Her laughter sparkled through him like droplets of springwater, making him a part of her joyous mood.

He lifted her out of the shower and, without taking his mouth from hers, wrapped a huge white bath towel about her, pulling it across at the front so that her arms were imprisoned. Then he imprisoned her again in both his own arms, but somehow he didn't feel any more in command of the situation than he had before. It was as though he were part of a preordained script, and even his assertion of power had come in the place she'd arranged for it.

He was dealing with a woman who knew him very well indeed, well enough to think three moves ahead of him, and that could be either thrilling or worrying, depending on your point of view. But for the moment, all that mattered was drying her down so that he could carry her to bed and do whatever else she'd planned for him.

Kaye was reveling in every moment. She knew she had Jack strung out to the edge, and she was going to make the most of it. The moment he tossed away the towel and picked her up she kissed him fiercely, enticing and tormenting him with her tongue, so that he nearly stumbled on the short journey out of the bathroom.

When they reached the bed it was she who pulled him down. His manhood was hard and powerful against her thighs, and she let it glide between them, squeezing it gently.

She had never loved his body so much, never been so thrilled by its strong contours. Despite his size he didn't carry an ounce of fat, and his active life had left his frame lean and honed. She explored him with her fingertips, caressing the long line of his thighs and hips, his broad back.

"Witch," he said softly.

"Mmm, you'd better believe it! I want you, Jack."

"That—was the impression I was getting."

"I mean, I want you *now*."

Nothing on earth could have stopped him after that. Her thighs fell apart, allowing him to enter her completely. No more teasing now, just the wholehearted acceptance of a woman for the lover of her choice. She was someone he'd never met before, a totally sensual, erotic creature, who lived in the darkness of passion where faces were hidden and only the truth could be seen.

And the truth lay in the way her back arched in a delirium of delight, and her hips thrust forward to meet his, giving and demanding with equal intensity. And because that was how she was, she made it the same for him. He'd never craved so much, taken so much, or given so much.

They climaxed at a moment of her deciding. Great as his control was, she overcame it at her pleasure, sending him into a fierce spin of delight that left him gasping, worn-out, yet ready for anything she wanted.

She wanted everything. With laughing eyes that gleamed at him through the darkness, she let him know that the night had barely begun. He met her challenge, letting her draw him in deeply, to the mysterious heart of her, where she seemed to offer everything, yet always revealed at the last minute that there was something more.

And gradually he began to understand. There was no end to this woman. There never would be, for she could reinvent herself every day and every night, yet still be the same.

As the first crack of gray crept in between the curtains he lay dazed with the knowledge that he'd had a great victory, or a triumphant, glorious defeat. Looking at his wife, sleeping like a baby in his arms, he wasn't sure he knew which.

Or that he would ever know.

Jack leaned back in his heavy leather chair, yawned and stretched. He'd made notes until his head ached, and now he was trying to think of something else to do.

He had an eerie feeling of déjà vu. It was only last night that he'd sat here in his office like this, finding more things that needed to be done so that he wouldn't have to go home. But in the end, he had gone. And Kaye had given him a welcome that had startled, exhilarated and shocked him.

There was the wonder of discovering that his demure wife could become a siren, taking the lead, enticing him, showing him how deeply he craved her. The full extent of that craving, never understood before, had alarmed him. It threatened the control that he needed in order to operate.

Even so, he could have coped, even enjoyed it, if it hadn't happened so soon after Rhoda had advised her daughter how to use her husband's desire to manipulate him.

There are a thousand ways to make a man sit up and beg.

He'd been so sure that his Kaye was above that. Yet within a few hours she'd turned into a seductress, confident of her power to enslave him, and willing to use it. For once he hadn't been in charge. Worse, he'd surrendered willingly, letting her lead him anywhere. It was only afterward that reaction had set in, and he became troubled.

For if Kaye had been trying to prove she could call the shots in bed, she'd succeeded in doing just that.

It had been years since anyone had called the shots to Jack Masefield, yet his demure little wife had managed it within hours of the overheard conversation that had—or should have—put him on his guard.

And just where had that guard been when she started her tricks? Nowhere. He'd been so startled, delighted, enthralled, dazzled, that he'd forgotten every word until it was too late.

She'd made him sit up and beg.

And now he was scared.

He'd risen early and hurried from the house, without even breakfast. He'd needed to put some distance between them, and think. Lord knew, he couldn't think when she was there.

But he hadn't done any thinking. He'd plunged into work in order to avoid thinking, and he'd managed it until the day was over and he was sitting alone in the quiet building, unable to shoo his fears away anymore.

He began making international calls. The time differences across the world were useful in extending his working day, and at one time he'd thought nothing of working almost through the night, sleeping a couple of hours, then rising bright and early to start again. He'd even been known to leave a lady's bed in the small hours to see if an urgent E-mail had arrived.

He'd never willingly left Kaye's bed. She'd always been ready for him, always eager to make love with a passion that contrasted with the quiet, almost diffident woman of the day. That contrast, too, had confused him, and never more than after the events of last night.

He made calls for a couple of hours. His head was fuzzy, which was unlike him, and he hadn't yet decided where to spend the night.

Then a very unwelcome voice came from the outer office. "Hallo? Anybody there?"

The woman who walked into the room was dressed with elegance and restraint. She was sparingly made-up and her hair was neat. For a moment Jack didn't recognize her, and when he did, he gasped.

"*Elsie?*"

"Good evening, Jack," she said coolly, coming right in.

"I thought you'd gone back to Monte Carlo," he said. He was on alert. He'd never seen his ex-wife look quite like this, and any surprise from Elsie usually meant that she was up to her tricks.

"I did go back, for a while. But I can't stay away from my little girl for long."

"Fine," he said, determined to speak pleasantly. "Georgy will be thrilled to see you. But why did you come here?"

"Because it's time you and I had a talk about the future, without that ninny you married sticking her oar in."

"If you really thought Kaye was a ninny you wouldn't be avoiding her," Jack said. Elsie scowled. "Kaye is my strength. While I've got her beside me you can do your worst."

"Don't be so sure of that. You were content to leave Georgy with me for years, because it suited you."

"She was a little girl then, and you kept her away from your dubious friends. Besides, you had help. I liked Valerie, and while she was there I didn't worry too much. Pity she left, and you didn't have the sense to replace her."

"You're very hard on me, Jack," Elsie said after a moment. "Do you know what it does to me, to know you're turning my child against me?"

"No way am I doing that. You're still her mother."

"Not now you've given her another one."

"Kaye isn't trying to push you out, and neither am I," Jack said, speaking kindly. "But Georgy's still a kid. She needs stability, and, let's face it, Elsie, you're not the most reliable person in the world."

"That's what you're going to tell the judge, is it?"

"Does it have to go in front of a judge? Can't we work out something reasonable?"

She gave a wan smile. "I know your idea of 'something reasonable.' It means doing what you want. You don't give an inch, Jack, and I can't fight you."

"Then let's not fight," he said gently. "We don't need to be enemies."

Elsie seemed to speak with difficulty. "It's just that—I tried so hard—I meant to be a good mother. I love her so much and you're taking her away from me...."

Suddenly she broke down, weeping bitterly. Jack stared at her, appalled. Years of fighting with his ex-wife had left him unprepared for the moment when she cracked. He knew her to be selfish, treacherous and totally without honor, but her heartbroken sobs upset him.

"Elsie, please," he said, slipping a friendly arm about her shoulders, "there's no need for this."

"I'm so lonely," she wept. "Oh, Jack, you don't know how lonely I am."

"Has François left you again?" he asked without malice.

"Everyone leaves me. I'm losing Georgy, but I always meant to be a good mother."

"I guess you did."

"You do believe me? That I did my best."

"Yes, I believe you," he said, not sure whether it was true, but wanting to comfort her.

"Yes, you do, don't you? *And so will the judge.*" She raised her head and looked him in the eye. The tears were gone, and only derision remained on her face. "I'll go into court, dressed as I am now, and cry my eyes out. Still fancy your chances against me?"

He stepped sharply away from her. "You..." he said softly, trying to find a word that described her.

"Forgot I used to be an actress, didn't you?" She gave a snigger. "You know me better than anyone, Jack. If I can fool you, I can fool anyone."

"Just another of your tricks," he said grimly.

"And you fell for it."

"Because, like an idiot, I want to believe the best of you," he said contemptuously. "That's a mistake I won't make again."

"You said something like that on the night you threw me out."

"I didn't throw you out," he snapped. "I just said I'd had enough of your sleeping around, and if you didn't change your ways, we were through. I'd have tried to patch it up, for Georgy's sake. But when I came home, you were gone."

"Sure I was. I couldn't live with a man who hated me."

"I never hated you, I just— Oh, the devil! What's the use of going through all that again?"

"You sure as hell didn't love me anymore by then."

"Don't play that game with me, Elsie, because I've got more ammunition than you have. You never loved me at all. You married me for what you thought I was worth, and the only reason you stuck with me so long was because I was worth more every year."

"And what did Kaye marry you for? Love? No way. I know how you broke up her wedding. She'd barely known you five minutes."

"There are gaps in your knowledge, Elsie. Kaye and I first met six years ago."

"Oh, please, I'm going to throw up. Next you'll be telling me she was in love with you for six years—*six years,* for God's sake!—and fell at your feet as soon as you turned up again. Get real. She needed another rich man for the sake of that pretty brother of hers."

"I think we'd better not discuss this," Jack said quietly. "I want you to leave."

"Fine. I'm on my way to see Georgy anyway."

"I don't want you going to my home tonight."

"Try to stop me." She turned and flounced out.

Jack ground his teeth, realizing that she was right. He slammed shut the door of his office and caught up with her by the elevator.

"Going to give me a lift?" she asked pertly. "Or must I hire a cab?"

"You can come with me," he said grimly. "I feel safer where I can keep my eye on you."

"Why, Jack, what a charming invitation."

He could tell that she was in high good humor at having disconcerted him. He clamped his mouth shut. His mood was murderous, and he didn't feel safe speaking to her.

When they'd driven for ten minutes in silence Elsie said, "Aren't you going to call your little wife? It wouldn't be fair to catch her unprepared."

He'd been thinking the same thing, but her jeering tone drove him to retort, "Kaye's not like you, Elsie. I can rely on her totally, and I never have to worry about what I'm going to find when I get home."

"My poor Jack! What a bore!"

"Cut it out. You wouldn't understand a woman like Kaye."

"If she's a woman, I understand her. We all have our own agenda. She's just more subtle than most in the way she presents it." When he didn't reply, she tittered. "Nothing to say? Oh, dear, did I hit a nerve?"

He would have died rather than admit that she had. Her words, coming so soon after Rhoda's, made his skin crawl. It was a moment before he could bring himself to speak.

"Now I think of it, I'm glad you'll catch Kaye unaware. You'll see things as they really are, see what kind of a home she makes for Georgy—a safe, decent home where she can live like a teenager, instead of being exposed to the kind of rotten crowd she met with you. Sneer all you want. I'm proud of my wife, and that's something I could never say when I was married to you."

That, he was glad to find, silenced her.

At last he swung into the drive at Maple Lodge, and headed for his usual place in the double garage. Subconsciously he noticed that something was different tonight, but he was too preoccupied with his thoughts to give it much attention.

The front door opened and Kaye came out to meet him, checking a little when she saw Elsie, but greeting her with determined politeness. "We all thought you were still in Monte Carlo," she said, smiling.

"You mean you hoped I was. I want to see Georgy."

"I wish you'd given us a little warning. She's in bed."

Because Kaye was alive to every nuance of Jack's

behavior, she saw his quick sigh of relief. She'd looked forward to this meeting all day, ever since awakening to find him gone. It had been disappointing not to find in him now any of the beautiful awareness that had possessed her all day, but she put that down to Elsie's presence.

"Bed, at half past ten?" Elsie exclaimed. "Don't tell me she agreed to that without argument."

"Actually, it was her idea," Kaye said. "I think she's started a cold."

"My poor little girl. Aren't you looking after her properly?"

"A girl of her age ought to be in bed by this hour," Kaye said, refusing to be disconcerted. "It's what I try for every night. Sometimes I even manage it."

Again there was the reaction on Jack's face, this time closer to triumph. She thought she could guess what they'd been talking about. Her spirits soared. It was for a moment like this that Jack had married her, and she was going to come through for him.

"Well, I've come a long way and I want to see her," Elsie insisted.

"Of course," Kaye said at once. "I'll go and awaken her. Perhaps you'd like some tea while you wait."

Elsie's eyes snapped. "You think you're so clever, coming the lady hostess over me." There was real hatred in her tone.

Kaye understood. Elsie was furious at finding no trouble to stir. Kaye's blood was up, and she felt it would be a pleasure to bring Georgy down, sleepy and virtuous, so that Elsie could see for herself how useless was her venom.

''Wait here,'' she said, and left the room.

Rhoda was passing through the hall as Kaye appeared. ''Where are you off to in such a hurry?'' she said.

''Elsie's here. I'm going to fetch Georgy.''

''But she'll be asleep by now.''

''It won't hurt her, and Elsie is her mother.''

''No, wait.'' Rhoda laid a hand on her daughter's arm. ''Why should you jump to attention every time that woman turns up? It makes me mad. You should stand up for yourself more.''

''Thanks, Mom,'' Kaye said, touched by Rhoda's unexpected show of concern, ''but I think I'd better give in about this. I know Jack doesn't want Elsie to be able to say we've been keeping Georgy from her.''

''Nonsense, tell her she can't just march in here. She ought to make an appointment. In fact, I'll tell her myself.''

She began to head for the living room, and Kaye was forced to place a restraining hand on her mother's arm. She was puzzled. It was strangely unlike Rhoda to take up the cudgels on her daughter's behalf. Yet even then Kaye had no suspicion of the truth.

''Leave it, Mom,'' she said. ''Let's just get this over with.''

She ran the rest of the way upstairs, leaving Rhoda staring after her. She didn't look back, and so failed to see her mother's expression full of dismay.

She knocked lightly on Georgy's door, but there was no response from within. After a moment she went in and approached the bed without putting on the light.

"Georgy," she said softly, "wake up."

Suddenly she became aware of the silence where there ought to have been breathing, and snapped on the light. The bed was empty. So was the room.

Chapter Ten

As Kaye stood, frozen with dismay, looking around Georgy's empty room, Rhoda's face came into her mind, and all the warning lights she'd failed to see before started flashing. It couldn't be true. And yet she knew it was.

"Mom."

Rhoda had slipped into the room behind her and was frantically shushing her. "Just keep quiet and nobody need know," she said.

"Where's Georgy?" Kaye demanded, her eyes kindling.

"Don't make a fuss. She only wanted a night out. You never give that girl any freedom."

Kaye's horror was mounting every moment. "Where is she, Mom? And where's Paul?"

"He took her out for a little bit of fun."

"They slipped out behind my back," she breathed. "And you knew. How could you do it?"

Jack appeared in the doorway. "What's taking so long? Where's Georgy?"

Kaye forced herself to face her husband. "She's not here. She made me think she was going to sleep and then she crept out of the house."

"Alone?" Jack's voice was sharp.

"No," Kaye said in despair. "With Paul."

As soon as he heard *with Paul,* Jack understood what had been strange about the garage. Kaye's car was missing.

"Where are they?" he asked in a hard voice.

"They just went for a little drive," Rhoda said petulantly.

"Where?" Jack's voice was harsher than Kaye had ever heard it.

"I don't know," Rhoda said with a shrug.

"What's up? What are you all whispering about?"

Everyone turned at the sound of Elsie's voice in the doorway. Her sharp eyes took in the whole scene, including the fact that there was no sign of Georgy.

"Where's my little girl?" she demanded. Her voice rose to a theatrical shriek. "Where is she?"

"Calm down, Elsie," Jack began.

"I'll calm down when I see my daughter. You can't keep her from me. Where are you hiding her?"

"Oh, shut up, you stupid woman!" Rhoda said. "Nobody's hiding her. She's gone out with my son. What's wrong with that?"

Elsie turned on her, her eyes glinting at the sight of an old foe. "What's wrong with that is that it's eleven o'clock, Georgy is only a child and your son is a crook.''

"Who do you think you are, calling my boy names?''

"There's a few names I'd like to call him. Does he know she's underage?''

"Of course he knows,'' Kaye said. "I promise you, Paul would never do her any harm—''

"He already has, snatching her from her bed like that—''

"Snatched, my eye!'' Rhoda scoffed. "You don't think he had to force that little madam, do you? She may be underage but she doesn't look it, and she certainly doesn't act it. And who's fault is that?''

"Your daughter's!'' Elsie said triumphantly. "Since she's the one looking after her.'' She swung around to Jack. "All that stuff I had to listen to—how Georgy had 'a safe, decent home.' And how Kaye was so reliable that you never had to worry about what you'd find.''

Kaye flinched at these words. Jack had paid her a tribute on the very night she'd let him down.

"Perhaps you should have been a bit more worried,'' Elsie went on remorselessly. "Little Miss Prim and Proper here's such a ruddy wonderful guardian that she's only let my little girl run off with her criminal brother.''

"Cut that out,'' Jack told her harshly. "Don't forget I arrived in Monte Carlo to find her alone in the house with Henri, a man with some very sinister connections.''

"But she was at home, wasn't she? Not out in some sleazy dive.''

"We don't know she's anywhere bad," Kaye said desperately. "They might have gone to a movie."

"And pigs might fly. That lowlife has taken her to a nightclub, I'll bet."

"You watch your tongue," Rhoda said, incensed.

"Who are you to give me orders?"

Sam and Bertie had slipped in, unnoticed by anyone. They watched the growing battle between the two women, their eyes gleaming.

"My money's on yours," Sam murmured. "She's got a nasty temper."

"Don't call Rhoda mine," Bertie growled. "I wouldn't have her as a gift."

"But she's going to make mincemeat out of Elsie," Sam pointed out. "And that's something I'm going to enjoy."

Rhoda was living up to his expectations. "I'll give you more than orders," she raged. "Talking about my son like that. I know what you are. I've heard the stories—drunken parties, men young enough to be your son, bringing your daughter up to be as degenerate as yourself. Is it any wonder she's out till all hours, dragging my innocent boy with her?"

Elsie gave a scream of laughter. "Innocent, my eye! I've danced with that lad. You can tell everything about a man by dancing with him, and I mean everything. If he's innocent, I'm a Mata flaming Hari."

"Why, you evil-tongued old—"

"Who the hell are you calling old?"

Sam and Bertie cheered like spectators at a prize-fight. But Kaye had no time to enjoy the humor of the situation. She was sick at heart at having failed Jack so badly, and a certain suspicion was tearing at her.

She darted away to her own room and went to the wardrobe where she kept Georgy's confiscated dress. Her worst fears were realized. It was missing.

Jack had followed her. "What is it?" he asked tensely.

"She bought a dress recently—bright red and cut very tight. I told her to return it, but it got torn. I brought it in here, but it's missing. If she's wearing that—oh, Jack, I—"

"Never mind," he said quickly. "We'll have the postmortems later. The first thing is to find them. Let's go quickly. I don't want Elsie trying to come with us."

As they left the house they could still hear the sound of raised voices from Georgy's room. In a short time Jack was swinging the car around and down the drive.

"They could be anywhere," Kaye said wretchedly.

"We'll try The Shining Star. They've heard of it because yesterday Bertie and Sam were telling the story of the night we chased them."

"I should have known there was something fishy when Georgy chose to go to bed early," Kaye said miserably. "She never does that."

"Don't blame yourself," Jack said. "She's as cunning as a cartload of monkeys."

Soon the glaring neon sign came into view. Jack parked right in front and they went in together. "Let's do this quietly," he said. "We'll enter as normal customers, and look around without attracting attention."

Kaye agreed. She was on edge, overwhelmed by how deeply she'd failed Jack, and although he'd said little so far, she knew he must be disappointed in her. She wasn't sure if she was more afraid of finding the young couple or not finding them.

In fact, they saw them almost at once. They were on the dance floor, gliding around smoochily, laughing into each other's eyes. Georgy was in the red dress, which sparkled as she moved. Her hair was swept up in a sophisticated style, her face was heavily made-up, and she looked ten years older than she was. Kaye saw the grim look about Jack's mouth. For once he was simply an outraged father.

They stayed back in the shadows until the youngsters had danced close to the edge of the floor. The music was coming to an end and they heard Georgy say, "Let's dance some more."

"Something to eat first," Paul replied. "Then we can—" He finished with a sharp intake of breath as he saw who was waiting for him.

"Paul, what are you...? *Daddy!*"

"There's no need for any trouble," Jack said quietly. "We're all going to leave together right now."

Even Georgy wasn't going to rebel against a certain note she heard in her father's voice. She gave them both a defiant glance, tossed her head and stalked out in front. Paul gave Kaye the sheepish look she knew so well. For once the sight didn't melt Kaye's heart.

"She just wanted to enjoy herself," he pleaded, "and she kept on at me to bring her here."

"Not very gallant to blame the lady," Kaye said coldly.

She turned on her heel and walked out, Paul trotting after her. "You know better than to bring a young girl to this place." She flung the words over her shoulder.

She pushed open the door into the street. Paul had to run to keep up with her. "Oh, come on, sis, don't make a fuss. There's no harm done."

Suddenly Kaye lost her temper and turned on him. "How *dare* you talk like that! Harm? You've no idea! Elsie turned up, demanding to see Georgy, and found her missing. Think of the ammunition you've given her! She called you 'that low-life,' and she was right."

"She's got a nerve!"

"It's not all she called you, and for once I agree with her."

"Oh, really? Well, I could tell you a thing or two about Madam Elsie. It may suit her to call me names now, but at your wedding she was all over me. Surely a handsome lad like me had a girlfriend? Didn't I know that older women had a lot to offer?"

"Shut up! You're disgusting!"

"All right, but I'm not the only one."

"Kaye, are you coming?" Jack called from the car.

"In a moment," she called. "I have some unfinished business here." She turned back to Paul. "You had no right to take my car, Paul. I want the keys back."

"Well, I—"

"This minute!"

"Sure." He handed them to her. "Perhaps it's best if you drive."

But she began to walk, not in the direction of her own car, but toward Jack. Georgy was already in the back seat, slumping down in a sulk. Kaye got in the front beside Jack and reached across him to touch the lock that secured every door. Paul, coming up close behind her, found the car locked against him.

"Hey, what about me?" he called.

Kaye wound down her window. "I don't want you in this car. I don't want you in my home. I don't want to see or hear from you again for a long time. Do I make myself plain?''

''All right, let me drive your car.''

''Get lost, Paul. Just get lost. I've had it with you.''

''But how am I to get back?'' he wailed.

''Walk. Not to Maple Lodge, because I won't let you in. You can walk right back home.''

''But it's miles and miles.''

''Good. It'll give you something to think of besides your own selfishness.''

''Just one night, and I'll leave in the morning.''

''Paul, watch my lips. I don't want to see you at Maple Lodge again, and neither does Jack—do you, Jack?''

This was so plainly an afterthought that, despite his anger, Jack couldn't help grinning. But he didn't answer. He was watching his wife with a curious look in his eyes.

''Jack,'' Paul pleaded, ''you wouldn't do this to me?''

Jack shrugged. ''We've both had our orders,'' he said. ''When Kaye's in this mood it's best to do as she says.''

He spoke lightly, but it was clear that something had changed. Kaye had found her voice. Paul's shocked face as he heard her pronounce his sentence proved that he knew it, too. The sister who'd protected him all his life had finally slammed the door, and nothing would ever be the same again.

There was silence on the way home. Kaye and Jack were both too wrung out to talk, and Georgy was in a furious temper. Kaye dreaded the scene when they reached home to find Elsie waiting to make the most of it. As they turned into the drive she could see Elsie on the front step, flanked by Rhoda, and the two old men.

But Jack nipped a scene in the bud. As soon as Georgy got out of the car he said in a voice that brooked no refusal, "Say good-night to your mother and get to bed."

Elsie looked as if she'd like to embark on a speech, but a glance from Jack silenced her. She looked daggers at him, but all she said was, "Leave it to me, darling. You're going to be back living with your mom very soon."

Georgy didn't answer at first. She seemed to be having trouble recognizing her mother. "What's that get-up?" she muttered, as if talking about her fancy dress.

"Where's Paul?" Rhoda demanded.

Jack made a gesture that referred her to Kaye. He was still looking at his wife in a new way, as though tonight he'd seen her for the first time.

"Paul's on his way home," Kaye said. "I told him not to come back here."

"She made him walk," Georgy cried. "She wouldn't even let him drive home in her car. And she said dreadful things to him."

"Walk?" Rhoda demanded, aghast. "You did a thing like that to your brother? You should be ashamed."

"The only thing I'm ashamed of is that I covered up for him so long," Kaye said. "It's over, Mom. It's time he stopped relying on me."

"You," Rhoda sneered. "What did you ever do for him?"

"Far too much," Kaye said quietly. "And most of

it was the wrong thing. I see that now. I've saved him from the consequences of his own actions, and I shouldn't have. This is where I stop. I'm sorry, Mom, but tomorrow I'd like you to leave, too.''

''I'll leave right now,'' Rhoda raged. ''I won't stay in a house where my boy isn't welcome.''

''In that case I'll call a taxi for you,'' Kaye said without hesitation.

Rhoda's jaw dropped. She was about to begin a furious tirade when she met Kaye's eyes and the words died on her lips. Caught in her own trap, she had no choice but to flounce off to start throwing her things together.

''Good riddance to bad rubbish,'' Elsie called after her.

''You can go in the same taxi,'' Kaye said calmly as she dialed the number. ''Say goodbye to Georgy now, and next time you want to see her, call me first.''

Like Rhoda, Elsie found that no words would come. Kaye's chilly assurance with its undertone of anger had astounded her. Perhaps she was even a little afraid of the unknown.

''Go and wash that muck off your face,'' Jack told his daughter in an iron voice, ''and don't let me see you again tonight.''

''Do as he says, darling,'' Elsie said, slipping back into her role as virtuous mother. ''And leave it to me to have you out of here.''

When Georgy had gone she turned on Jack. ''Don't think you've won. After tonight's little shindig I'll have no trouble getting the law on my side. And it's *her* you'll have to thank.'' She jabbed a finger at Kaye.

''Leave, Elsie,'' Jack told her coldly. ''Just leave.''

The cab arrived as Rhoda came downstairs. She flung Kaye a glance of loathing and stalked out. Elsie, in response to a jerk of Jack's head, followed her. The two women sat in freezing silence, as far away as possible from each other.

When they were gone Bertie let out an exultant roar. "That's my girl!" he cried, seizing Kaye in a bear hug. "I always knew you'd stand up to her one day."

"I should have done it years ago," she agreed. "I've seen a lot of things clearly tonight. A lot of things," she repeated in a low voice.

She closed the front door and shot the bolts home. The gesture had the effect of drawing a line under the incident. The disastrous evening was over. There was no more to be said.

"I'm going to bed," Kaye said.

"I'll be up later." Jack sounded abstracted.

When Kaye had gone Sam asked in a bewildered voice, "Who was that?"

"I don't know," Jack said. "I think it was my wife, but I'm not sure anymore."

Kaye was ready for bed when Jack entered her room, in his robe. She went to him and gave him a hug. She wanted to take him to bed, not romping like last night, but tenderly, in comfort and reassurance. But although he returned her hug it was only faintly, as though his mind were elsewhere.

"What is it?" she asked. "Are you sure you're not angry with me?"

"Of course not," he said quickly. "Besides, that's in the past. It's just that so much has happened tonight—I can't get my head together—"

Kaye went to slip her arms about his neck, but backed off before the look in his eyes. It was the same distant look she'd seen there too often in the first month of their marriage, and it meant he was hiding from her.

"What is it, Jack? There's something you're not telling me."

"It's nothing. I'm just tired."

"No, it's more than that."

"I just feel that— I'm sorry, I made a bit of a fool of myself. I thought a lot of stupid things. I should have known you better."

"You don't know me at all," she said lightly. "You're always proving it."

"You're right, or I'd never have believed—"

"Oh, Jack." She sighed. "What crime have I committed inside your head? Is it as bad as last time?"

Her tolerant tone tempted him to an act that he afterward saw was madness. "Much worse," he said. "I came home early yesterday and heard your mother in full flow."

"But you didn't get here until late," she said, puzzled and trying not to feel the cold hand gripping her stomach.

"That was the second time. I had to go away and think."

"And what did you decide?" Kaye asked, letting her hands drop.

"Nothing. I was confused, and you confused me still more. You've never been like that before, either in bed or out."

"And you remembered what you heard my mother say," she said quietly.

"Kaye, I went off my head. I'm only telling you this because I know I can trust you."

"Thanks for the compliment," she flashed. "What a pity I can't trust you to think the best of me."

"Kaye, please—"

"That's why you stayed away tonight, isn't it? You wanted to work out what I'd really been doing last night. Was it genuine, or was I trying to make you 'sit up and beg'? I believe that was my mother's charming phrase. If Elsie hadn't turned up you'd have stayed away all night, judging me by the lowest standards you can imagine. I think I've earned better than that from you, Jack."

"Kaye, please—I thought things I had no right to, but only briefly. I know I can trust you. That's why I told Elsie I wasn't afraid to come home without warning. I meant it. Don't crucify me because I lost my head for a moment."

He looked so pale and wrung out that she couldn't go on. "It doesn't matter," she said tiredly. "Too much has been said already tonight. We'll pretend it didn't happen."

She turned away. Jack came after her and put his hands on her shoulders. "Thank you," he said. "I knew you'd understand."

"Oh, yes, I understand a lot," she said with a little sigh. "I think I'll go to bed now. I'm very tired. I'd rather you didn't stay. Good night, Jack."

"Good night," he said after a long moment.

Elsie made her move at once. Kaye was with Jack when the letter arrived, and saw him go pale as he read it. "What's happened?" she asked urgently.

"Elsie's playing her ace," he said in a harsh voice. "She's started legal proceedings to get Georgy back."

"She hinted at that," Kaye said, "but I hoped it was just big talk."

"I'm afraid she wasn't bluffing. She's hired Elroy Hamblin."

Kaye paled at the name of the famous lawyer. He'd made a career out of high-profile cases, and he was prepared to pull every dirty trick in the book to ensure his own success. He was widely despised, but he delivered.

"How good is your lawyer?"

"Andrew is brilliant at company law. That's his speciality. But I don't know who to go to for this."

"Andrew will know," Kaye pointed out practically. "Call him now."

He did so. Andrew Morgan promised to get him a name, and was as good as his word.

"Charles Sedgeway," Jack said, hanging up. "I've heard of him. He's good. Whether he's a match for Hamblin—I don't know." He sighed.

"Don't go to meet trouble," Kaye said urgently. "This is where we fight back."

She squeezed his hand, but inwardly she was more concerned than she wanted him to know. A meeting with Sedgeway only increased her worries.

"She's playing it very, very cleverly," he said, regarding Jack and Kaye sitting uneasily in his office. "She's booked into a small, rather dull hotel and letting it be known, discreetly, that she can't afford anything better."

"She can afford the Ritz on what I pay her," Jack said angrily.

"You're still paying her alimony? What about her other 'companions'?"

"She never married any of them," Jack pointed out. "And the money was really for Georgy."

"Maybe that's why she's fighting so hard," Kaye said. "She's afraid she'll lose out financially."

"Let her know there'll be no changes," Jack said eagerly.

They went home full of hope, but it was immediately dashed. Hamblin wrote by return of post expressing his client's "deep distress" at the suggestion that her motives were in any way financial.

"Why is she doing this?" Jack cried, tearing his hair. "Don't tell me she loves Georgy. She's incapable of love."

"She's doing it because she hates you," Bertie said shrewdly.

"I've never given her any cause to hate me," Jack protested.

"She treated you badly, but it didn't destroy you. It destroyed her. She did everything for money and now money is all she has left. She's getting older and she's alone, while you're starting a new life with Kaye. She really hates you, Jack."

"Yes," he said slowly. "I guess she does."

He didn't respond to Bertie's remark about Kaye. On the surface their life continued unchanged. The trouble seethed underneath, all the more dangerous for that. She'd discovered that she could actually be angry with Jack, something she'd once have thought impossible. Her memories of that magnificent night had been wonderful, and he'd spoiled them in retrospect.

But she kept these thoughts to herself, for the moment. He had enough to worry him, and the time wasn't right.

When she found him one day setting down the telephone with a heavy look on his face she thought Elsie had come up with a new trick. "Jack, tell me what's the matter, please," she said quickly.

He sighed. "I'd rather not have to, but there's no way out. It's Paul."

They'd heard nothing of Paul since the night Kaye had left him to walk home. Rhoda had telephoned her with a bitter tirade about coming across him, weary and footsore, as she went home in the taxi, but from Paul himself, not a word.

Jack hadn't, as Kaye half expected, ordered his dismissal from North's, but now he said, "I'm afraid I can't keep him in that job."

"What's happened?"

"He didn't turn up for work last Monday. Apparently he took the car for a weekend jaunt with some friends, and allowed them to drive it. One of them smashed it against a tree. Nobody was hurt, but the car's a write-off. And since this 'friend' of Paul's was disqualified from driving, the insurers won't pay out.

"When Paul realized the trouble he was in, he simply ran away and hid. I had to discover the truth bit by bit."

Kaye gave a long sigh, and rested her forehead in her hands.

"I'm sorry, Kaye," he said gently. "I did my best."

"I know you did. Paul's as he is, and I guess he isn't going to change. Oh, Jack, what's going to become of him?"

"I dread to think, but you mustn't go back on your

resolution to be firm with him. He's got to make the effort himself.''

''I know, but you can't stop loving people to order. I only wish you could.'' She gave a sad little laugh. ''Think how much easier life would be.''

''Yes,'' he agreed, half to himself.

Kaye awoke in the early hours to find Jack sitting by her window, looking out through a crack between the curtains. He wore only his robe, and Kaye studied him in the shaft of light, wishing the hint of his nakedness didn't affect her so powerfully. It was two weeks since their last lovemaking, the night of her ill-fated seduction, and this was the first time he'd been in her room since then. It was as though they were both waiting for something to happen, and neither knew what it was, or how to bring it about.

''Has something happened that I don't know about?'' she asked, getting out of bed and going to him.

''No, I've just been doing some thinking. None of this would have happened if I'd been a better father.''

''It's not your fault that you haven't seen more of Georgy.''

''Maybe it is. I should have done more, sooner. I've tried to be a good father. I love her. I've kept in touch, brought her presents, always remembered her birthday and listened when she wanted to talk. We spent hours on the phone, and I let myself think that was enough. But it takes more than a huge phone bill to make a good father.''

''A lot of men don't even bother to spend time talk-

ing to their teenage daughters,'' she said lightly to
encourage him.

"Don't let me off too easily. I have a lot to feel
guilty about. I've always known the kind of woman
Elsie is. I should have brought Georgy to live with me
long ago, but I didn't because—"

"Because?"

"Because I didn't want to interrupt my pleasant,
careless life to take responsibility for a growing girl,"
he said heavily. "I should have given her a home, but
I settled for being a father the easy way."

"But she's a wonderful kid, and you brought her to
live with you before any harm was done."

"Thanks to you," he said, twining her fingers in
his. "The best thing I ever did was to marry you. I've
turned over a new leaf. With your help I'm going to
be a better father."

"You love Georgy. That's the main thing."

"It's not enough. I make mistakes, but you can
show me the way." He leaned his head against her.
"I need you, Kaye," he whispered. "I need your
strength. Until recently I didn't even know how strong
you are, but I want you fighting on my side. Elsie's
making war, and you're the only one who knows how
to deal with her."

If Jack had been a subtle man he might have been
able to voice the unease that had possessed him since
he'd seen her assert herself against the selfish claims
of others. He might even have found the words for his
growing fear that his own claims were selfish, and his
dread at the thought of the coming day when she
would tell him, too, to take his possessive claws out
of her life.

But he wasn't subtle. He was simply a great-hearted, plain-dealing man who coped with things by charging at them headlong. "Like a bull at a gate," Sam had once caustically complained, and certainly Sam would have groaned if he'd heard his son making a mess of things now.

Kaye, listening closely for words of love, heard *Georgy, mistakes, need* and *help.* When she was sure Jack wasn't going to say what her heart longed to hear she closed her eyes, fighting back the tears. At last she put her arms about him.

"It's all right, Jack. I'm always here for you. You know that."

Jack, listening closely for words of love, heard only the kindly tones Kaye used to people who sucked her dry, and from whom she was freeing herself. He put his own arms about her, and they sat together in silence, holding each other tightly, yet far apart in their fear.

Chapter Eleven

Kaye was dismayed, but not entirely surprised, to realize that Georgy now saw herself as the heroine of a tragic love story. "You've warned Paul off, haven't you?" she demanded sulkily one day.

"Certainly I did," Kaye said briskly. "You heard me."

"No, I mean since then. You've told him to stay away from me. Or Dad has."

"Neither of us has."

"Then why hasn't he called me?"

"Because he has a shrewd sense of self-preservation. I wish you'd stop this, Georgy. You're not Juliet to his Romeo, even if he does look the part."

"Has he called you?"

"No."

Kaye had half expected Paul to call her when he

lost his job, but there was no word, and she tried to persuade herself that this was a good sign. It meant he was learning to stand on his own feet. Secretly she felt the silence was ominous.

But, however tempted, she refused to make the first move. Things had changed. She wasn't a soft touch for Paul anymore, and it wouldn't be kind to let him think otherwise.

When she did see him it came as a surprise. Emerging from a stint at the nursery one afternoon, she found Paul leaning against her car. He gave a cheeky little wave when he saw her.

"You got home safely, then?" she said, surveying him.

"Much you care! You didn't even call to ask."

"Mom told me she collected you on the road. I knew you'd land on your feet, Paul. You always do."

"Do you mind not talking about feet?" he asked with a theatrical wince. "I was limping for a week afterward."

She hadn't greeted him in her usual way, with a hug, and this seemed to disconcert him. "You wouldn't like to treat your favorite little brother to a meal, would you?" he asked, at his most winning.

"There's a burger bar over the way," she said, heading out of the parking lot.

He trotted after her. "I was hoping for a thick steak with French fries and mushrooms, and a bottle of—"

"The way I feel about you at the moment you're lucky to get a burger."

She noticed that he was dressed in old jeans and sweater, which was unusual for Paul. He caught her glance and gave a sheepish shrug.

When they were sitting down, with food in front of them, she asked, "How have you been?"

He grimaced. "Oh, so-so! I had to pack the job in. I couldn't stand working for Lionel North. He couldn't organize a booze-up in a brewery. I had some great plans for reorganizing the place and he didn't want to know."

"But you were supposed to be selling socks."

"I'm an ideas man. If he'd listened to me he could have doubled his profit. Anyway, I told him I couldn't work for a man with such limited vision. He begged me to stay, but I told him it wasn't on."

Kaye sat in silence, her heart sinking at the desperate edge in his voice. "How's Mom?" she asked at last.

"Pretty unbearable. She nags me all the time, and you should hear some of the things she says about you."

"I can imagine. She thought Jack would be easy to manipulate, but I won't let that happen."

"She thought he'd do something for me," Paul said sulkily.

"He did do something for you," Kaye said angrily. "He's part owner of North's. That's how you got the job. And you blew it."

Several expressions flitted across Paul's face—dismay, outrage, disbelief, certainty and finally horror as he realized how much she must know about his dismissal.

"Oh, hell!" he said. "Still, you can make him give me another chance."

"I couldn't. Nobody makes Jack do anything."

"Please, Kaye, he'd do it for you."

"Paul, listen, Jack only married me to get Elsie off his back. I'm useful to him. That's why he won't let my family batten off him, even if I'd ask him, which I won't."

"Yes, you dropped us fast enough when you got your escape route, didn't you?"

"That's not fair—"

"I'm not blaming you, sis. If someone would wave a magic wand and get me away from Mom, I'd be off like a shot."

"That's not very nice to her," Kaye said, discovering that it was actually possible to feel sorry for Rhoda.

"Well, she won't get off my back. Nag, nag—tidy your room—nag, nag—get a job—nag, nag."

"Paul, most lads of your age are eager to get out of their mother's house and make their own way."

"Well, I'd get out if I could afford it. You don't think I like living there, do you?"

"So get a job, stick with it and find your own place. If Mom nags it's probably because she's tired of supporting you."

"She's turned against me, Kaye. My own mother's turned against me."

"Stop being melodramatic," she told him sternly. "Mom would never do that."

"Oh, no? She only sold all my best clothes. That's why I'm in rags today. Just to raise a few measly pounds."

"*Mom* did that? To you?" It was as though the world had turned upside down.

"Yes. She was really nasty. Just because I didn't

have any money to pay my credit card. It wasn't my fault."

Kaye had a sudden, dismayed vision of her brother in a few years' time, when his youth began to fade, and the futility and weakness in his face could no longer be hidden. When that time came he would still be saying, "It wasn't my fault." And wondering why nobody believed it.

"What's going to happen to you?" She sighed in despair.

He shrugged. "You tell me. You could help me, but you don't want to."

"I've told you—"

"Yes, but I don't believe it. Jack's crazy about you, d'you think I don't know that?"

He was wrong, of course, and it was absurd that his casual words should make her heart beat faster. What could Paul know about it?

"I don't see how you can be so sure," she said, trying to sound casual.

"Because I've seen the way he looks at you when he thinks nobody's watching him. It's kind of—I don't know—like he's caressing you with his eyes."

The sudden poetical phrase pulled her up short. Paul must have read it somewhere. He was saying what he guessed she wanted to hear, hoping there would be something in it for him.

His next words seemed confirmation. "How's Georgy? Missing me?"

"Forget Georgy. Jack will never allow you near her again, and without his approval…" She shrugged.

"She's no use to me," Paul finished bluntly. "You're right. A busted flush."

Kaye lost her temper. "You only think of yourself, don't you?" she said furiously. "You never give a thought to how your actions affect other people. What do you think it looked like when Elsie found Georgy out nightclubbing with my brother, a convicted criminal?"

"Don't exaggerate. A bit of shoplifting—"

"When Elsie's finished it's going to look like grand larceny, fraud, corruption and stealing the crown jewels. You have a police record, and if it wasn't for me Georgy would never have met you. That's going to look wonderful when she brings it out in court."

"What's all this talk about court?"

"Elsie's started legal proceedings. It's not funny," she said indignantly as he gave a choke of laughter.

"It is, in a way. Elsie, doing her devoted-mother act. Why does she bother? She's not the maternal type."

"Georgy's a weapon against Jack. Also, the boyfriend has left her for a younger woman and she needs something to fill the gap."

"Surely the court will see through her?"

"Elsie's an actress, so she might just manage to be convincing. Plus, she's got a very good lawyer. She might win, and if she does, I'll never forgive you."

"That's right, blame me."

He fell silent, and Kaye let him get on with his sulk. At last he said, "Maybe I can solve your problems and mine, all in one go."

"What do you mean?"

He gave her a mischievous grin. "Never mind. I want to think this over awhile first."

She let it pass. She knew Paul in his "big-talking"

moods. He would say anything to get what he wanted, and forget every word afterward. He confirmed this a moment later by producing his latest credit card statement and saying, in his most winning voice, ''Kaye, darling, couldn't you—just this once...?''

''You've really got a nerve. You'll never change, will you?''

''Why should I change? Go on, it's peanuts to you.''

''Sorry, Paul, but I'm a 'busted flush,' too. Big sister is going to let you sink or swim this time.''

Driving home, she felt depressed and wondered why she'd told him so much. But she was lonely. On the surface she seemed to have everything to make her happy. She was married to the man she loved, and he was good to her. But he'd laid out the terms on the night he opened his heart to her and she'd found need there, but not love. That was their life now, and she was beginning to believe that there would never be any other.

The tension in the household was becoming almost palpable. Jack was bombarded by letters from Elsie's lawyer and from his own. Charles Sedgeway's outlook was gloomy. If Elsie could keep up her sedate appearance and her respectable act, her chances looked good.

''She's come up with a new trick,'' Jack said gloomily one morning. ''Nobody knows where she is. Even Hamblin can't contact her. Or so he says.''

''You mean she's vanished?''

''If only she would. No, she just enjoys the thought of us all running around in circles. Whenever I call her hotel she's always out, but she's still registered there. She'll surface when it suits her. By the way, Georgy's in a stew about something. I can't get any sense out of her. Maybe you can.''

Kaye hurried up to the girl's room. Georgy looked up with sullen eyes, and it seemed to Kaye that she'd been crying. "What's up?" she asked gently. "Can't you tell me?''

Georgy's lower lip wobbled. "It's all your fault," she said.

Kaye spoke cheerfully. "Sure it is. Let's take that as read, and you tell me what my crime is this time.''

"You drove Paul away, you and Dad. He might have vanished off the face of the earth, and you wouldn't care.''

"Of course he hasn't vanished off the face of the earth.''

"Then where is he? Where's he gone?''

"What are you talking about, Georgy?" Kaye asked, frowning. "He hasn't gone anywhere.''

"I called him at home. Your mom says she came home two days ago and found the house empty.''

Kaye frowned. "I knew nothing of this, honestly. I'm sure he's only gone to see some friends.''

Kaye tried calling her mother's number, but there was no reply. She continued calling for the next two hours, without success. "Perhaps I should drive over and see if she's all right," she said worriedly to Jack.

"But she probably isn't at home," he pointed out. "If she were, she'd answer the phone, in case it was Paul.''

"That's true.''

Sam and Bertie appeared, looking excited. "There's a taxi drawing up," Sam said. "My God, it's Rhoda!''

"I'm out of here," Bertie said at once.

"Stay where you are," Sam ordered. "I'll protect you with my life."

Kaye pulled open the front door to her mother. Rhoda's face was very pale, there were black smudges under her eyes and she regarded her daughter with hostility.

"Is he here?" she demanded without preamble. *"Is Paul here?"*

"Paul? No, of course not. You must know he isn't welcome in this house."

"But I know you took him to lunch. I thought perhaps you'd given him money to go away."

"No, I refused to give him any money."

"Then where is he? How can he just vanish like this?"

"Come and have some tea," Kaye said. "And tell me what happened."

Jack and Georgy joined them in the kitchen. Sam and Bertie hovered just outside. While she made the tea she was aware of Rhoda's eyes on her, full of a mixture of anger and curiosity. It made her uncomfortable.

"He didn't even say goodbye," Rhoda complained. "Didn't leave a letter, not a word—to me, who's done everything for him."

Kaye pitied her too deeply to say anything. When she handed Rhoda her tea her mother accepted it with a weary shrug. The fight seemed to have drained out of her.

"He walked out of that job, you know," she said. "I told him he was crazy, but he said he couldn't work for that man anymore." After a moment she looked up to find Kaye regarding her with compassion. "They fired him, didn't they?" she said, sighing.

"I'm afraid so," Kaye said. Briefly she explained about the car. She spoke as gently as she could. She had no wish to hurt her mother. But Rhoda seemed beyond pain. For years she'd blinded herself to the truth about her darling, but now it all seemed to have overwhelmed her at once.

"Last time I saw him, he said you'd sold his clothes," Kaye added, remembering.

"It was just after he lost the job. He kept on spending money, and the bills were coming in. I thought I could make him face reality, but he didn't listen. It just made him hate me."

Kaye tried to think of something to say, but only the truth would do, and the truth was too cruel.

"We had rows," Rhoda said. "And I'd look in his eyes and see that he hated me."

She sounded bewildered. All the years of spoiling him, overlooking his faults, making him her king, all come to this.

The telephone shrilled. Kaye answered it and received a shock.

"Hi, sis!" Paul had never sounded chirpier.

"Paul, where on earth are you?" she demanded.

"In Monte Carlo."

As soon as he said it Kaye knew the whole truth, knew that Paul would do anything rather than work for a living, knew how he'd intended to "solve her problems." In fact, it should have been obvious as soon as he and Elsie both disappeared at the same time. But who would have expected something so outrageous—even from this pair?

"What are you doing there?" she asked carefully.

"I'll give you one guess. I went to see Elsie, to apologize for that night, and...one thing just led to another."

"Which you always meant to happen."

"Of course. Why not? She's loaded."

"I can't believe you've done this," she breathed.

"Oh, come on, sis, take your moral hat off. I've got you out of a hole. Elsie's gone right off the idea of having Georgy back. She's taken fifteen years off her age, and now that I'm here the last thing she wants is a daughter who looks grown-up. Anyway, what court would rule in her favor now?"

It was all true. Dazed, Kaye realized that Paul's action, selfish and vulgar though it might be, had swept away every practical problem.

"I told you I'd get you off the hook," he said cheerily. "You didn't believe me, but I did it. Call it my thank-you for all you've ever done for me."

"What's he saying?" Rhoda demanded. "Where is he? Give me that phone."

Kaye handed it to her and went to stand by Jack and Georgy.

"What's happened?" Jack asked, alarmed by her shocked face.

"Paul's gone to Monte Carlo," Kaye said, her eyes on Georgy. She touched the girl's arm gently. "He's with Elsie."

"Mom?" Georgy said slowly. "Paul's living with Mom?"

"I'm afraid so."

Her heart was torn with compassion for the girl, little more than a child, who'd received such an ugly shock. But she hadn't allowed for Georgy's upbringing, or the natural resilience of youth. Instead of bursting into tears, Georgy expressed her feelings in one forceful word.

"Yuck!"

"I'm sorry, darling," Jack said, his arm about her shoulders. "I know you were fond of him—"

"Fond of him? Daddy, he's a nerd."

Kaye blinked. "I beg your pardon?"

"I had to *make* him take me out that night. He kept worrying in case we got caught. And only a nerd would let you lock him out of the car the way you did. I ask you!"

"Hey, what became of *Romeo and Juliet?*" Kaye demanded.

"Oh, well…" Georgy's shrug implied that there were conventions to these things, that sheer self-respect demanded that she conceal her disillusionment with Paul from her "olds."

"Still," Jack said cautiously, "I know it's not nice for you to think of your mother—"

Georgy shrugged. "She's had toyboys before. At least Paul's not as young as Nico."

"That's fortunate," Jack said faintly.

Rhoda had reached the stage of shouting.

"That woman insulted me and you're shacking up with her? You ought to be ashamed of yourself. You get right back here— Don't you talk to me like that—"

"Excuse me," Georgy said, taking the receiver from Rhoda's hand. "Paul? Get a life!"

She hung up.

Chapter Twelve

The household was jubilant. After the long anxiety the nightmare was over. It took one meeting with Charles Sedgeway to confirm what they already knew.

"Mrs. Masefield has withdrawn her application for custody," he said, showing them the letter, "which, in any case, couldn't have been successful after this. It all seems to have worked out pretty neatly."

Jack and Kaye celebrated with a champagne lunch and agreed that it had, indeed, worked out neatly. For a couple of hours they smiled and said all the right things, but secretly each was becoming aware of a sense of dismay.

"What am I doing here?" Kaye asked Bertie. "Elsie's off the scene, and Georgy's happy to stay here now."

"She's still going to need a good mother," Bertie pointed out.

"Yes, but she's growing up so fast—I was looking forward to Jack and I taking her on vacation, but she's got this school friend whose parents are cruising the Norwegian fjords, and they've invited Georgy to fly out and join them. She wants to go, and Jack's agreed."

"But Jack still needs you, darling," Bertie said.

"Does he?" Kaye asked wistfully. "What for?"

"Dad!" Georgy's head appeared around Jack's bedroom door.

"The answer's no," he said hastily.

"But you don't know what I want."

"When you use that wheedling tone my antennae go into alarm mode," he said wryly. "What do you want that I'm not going to like you wanting?"

"You've got a suspicious mind." Georgy came right into the room and bounced on the bed.

"It's the effect of living with you."

"I'm packing for Norway. I only want to borrow your olive green silk scarf. It'll look great if I wear it as a belt with my cream dress."

"If that's really all, yes, you can. It should be in one of those drawers, over there."

Georgy began to turn out the drawers, tossing the contents onto the bed with gay abandon. "Don't worry, I'll put it all back afterward," she assured him.

"I was afraid of that," he said with a grin.

"Honestly, anybody would think I was untidy or something," Georgy complained. "Are you sure it's in this drawer?"

"I said *one* of those drawers."

"Well, it isn't—hey! What are you doing with this? Kaye never lets it out of her sight."

"What's that?" Jack regarded something Georgy was holding up.

"It's Kaye's little wooden horse. Does she know you've got it?"

"That's not Kaye's. It's mine."

"Are you sure? It looks like hers."

"They're identical. We bought them together."

"When? Last week? Last month?"

"Six years ago, on Singleton. I took her to dinner to thank her for coping with the little horror that you were then—"

"As opposed to the big horror that I am now," Georgy said, much entertained.

Jack tweaked her nose fondly. "As you say. A souvenir seller came to our table and I bought Kaye one of these little horses. So she bought me one just like it."

"And you've cherished it all these years," Georgy said dramatically. "And to think I had you down as a dreary old stick-in-the-mud."

"Any more out of you and you can forget that scarf," Jack said, sounding harassed.

"Oh, Dad, don't be a spoilsport. You've both kept them. That's the most romantic thing I've ever heard."

"You mean Kaye's still got hers?" Jack asked casually.

"I know she has. I've seen it. Only for a moment, because she snatched it out of sight and hid it away." A flash of insight made her say, "*She* didn't forget she still had it."

"I didn't exactly forget—at least, I did for some

time. I found it recently. Do me a favor, Georgy—you never saw this. Not a word to Kaye.''

''But she'd really like to know.''

''I'm not so sure.'' He had a sudden impulse to confide in her. Despite her youth she had the female point of view, and possibly understood Kaye better than he did himself. ''I never really know what she's thinking,'' he admitted.

''What does that matter, as long as you know what she's feeling?''

''I'm not sure about that, either. When people marry as we did—on the spur of the moment, not really knowing each other, each with their own agenda—''

''Own agenda?'' she echoed, frowning.

''I married her for your sake, she married me for Paul's sake.''

''Oh, *Dad!*'' she said with youthful scorn. ''Kaye married you because she was nuts about you. I saw it from the start, and even if I hadn't, I'd have known when you had your boating accident.''

''What do you mean by that?''

''She was devastated. When your boat turned over I thought she was going to faint. She was crying as much as I was, and when they brought you on board, she knelt beside you saying your name over and over—she was in a terrible state, Dad. Honest. Dad?''

''Er, yes—'' he said, startled.

''You were miles away.''

''Keep this under your hat, Georgy,'' he said with an effort. ''Things don't always mean what we hope—that is, what they seem.''

Georgy became very worldly-wise. ''I can tell when a woman's in love, Dad. Even if you can't.''

"That's enough out of you, cheeky. And remember what I said."

"My lips are sealed." She darted out, clutching the scarf.

Left alone, Jack picked up the little horse and held it in his palm. For a moment he was back on Singleton, looking at Kaye across the table, seeing her glow with adoration. He should have heeded the warning and never come so close to making love with her, but she'd charmed him out of his mind.

Thank God he'd been able to stop himself in time. Even so, he knew he'd hurt her feelings cruelly. She'd loved him. He could still hear her sobbing words, *I'll never love anyone but you.*

He'd dismissed it as the delusion of a child. But now another memory came to stand beside it. As he lay semiconscious on the deck after the boat crash, her voice had whispered to him out of the darkness. *I love you. I've always loved you.*

He hadn't been certain he heard the words. And when she hadn't come to the hospital in the ambulance with him, he knew he'd only imagined them. Now he wasn't so sure.

He saw her again as she'd been that night in the Caribbean, radiant. Everything about her was shining—her innocence, her warmth, her honesty. He'd known then that she was the most honest person in the world. How had he come to forget what she was really like?

All this time, since their marriage, he'd held off from her. Even when they'd found ecstatic passion in each other's arms he'd kept some part of himself aloof, waiting for the moment of disillusionment, almost willing it to happen, because that way he was still in control. He'd suspected her of double motives on the flimsiest of evidence, because to believe in her was to take a risk, and he'd told himself that as long as he treated her well, his cynical thoughts couldn't hurt her. It had seemed like common sense at the time, but now it looked like the action of a coward.

Jack had been called many things, from an intrepid hero to a reckless fool. But this was the first time he'd been called a coward, and the fact that he was his own accuser didn't make it any more pleasant.

It seemed impossible for one young girl to pack for a vacation without turning the whole house upside down. To Jack's relief, the turmoil prevented anyone noticing that he was preoccupied with his own thoughts. Even Kaye didn't seem to notice, which surprised him, because usually she noticed everything. But Kaye, too, was preoccupied these days. Sometimes it almost seemed that she was eager not to be alone with him. On the night before Georgy's departure Kaye arrived home late, when the others had almost finished eating.

"You've been visiting your mother again, haven't you?" Jack asked as he helped her off with her coat.

"Yes, I'm sorry I'm late. She kept making excuses to keep me there, and I couldn't bear to walk out and leave her alone in that empty house."

"All the charm of novelty, in fact. Kaye, I don't mean to be unkind, but you know, don't you, that if Paul came back tomorrow—"

"He isn't going to."

"That doesn't change the fact that she's making use of you."

"I know, but what can I do? She's so lonely it's scary, and she needs me at last."

"Sorry to sound like a curmudgeon."

"You're not a curmudgeon. I noticed a large deposit had suddenly arrived in my bank account—"

"Well, I guess Paul left debts, and Rhoda can't afford to pay them. So you'll do it for her."

"Thank you, anyway. It'll be for the last time."

"Yes, now he'll be Elsie's responsibility. Good luck to them both!"

Sam and Bertie came out of the dining room, and Bertie swept her off to supper. Sam looked at his son curiously.

"All right, son?"

"Yes, I suppose so," he said wryly. "It's just that I thought perhaps my turn had come. Well, I'm the fool! Come on, Sam, let's go and finish eating."

Next morning Jack and Georgy set off for the airport, where she would catch the plane for Norway. Kaye had chosen to stay behind. Georgy said goodbye to her with a warm hug that would have seemed impossible only a short time ago. Kaye and her two elderly cavaliers stood on the step, waving until the car was out of sight.

They watched her without seeming to, noticing how the smile faded from her face when her husband was gone, and the sad look that was left behind.

"See that?" Sam asked when Kaye had walked away.

"I saw it."

"Things aren't right."

"She thinks he doesn't need her anymore."

Sam made a sound perilously close to a snort. "I've given up waiting for those two to sort themselves out. It's time for action."

"But I don't want Kaye to think me an interfering old fool."

"I've never been afraid to be called an interfering old fool," Sam said robustly. "Been one all my life. Too late to stop now."

"But what can we do?" Bertie asked.

Sam told him.

It was one of Kaye's favorite tasks to feed the gold-fish in the huge ornamental pond in the garden. They were fat and greedy and came eagerly to the side to greet her.

Bertie was there, sitting on a stone bench, staring into the water. Kaye gave him a kiss and knelt on the flagstones.

"It's nice to see Georgy getting on so well with Jack," she mused. "They seem so at ease with each other now, don't you think, Grandpa? Grandpa?"

"I'm sorry, darling," Bertie said, apparently coming out of a dream. "What did you say?"

"Grandpa, are you all right?"

"Of course I am." He gave her a smile that was slightly too bright to be convincing.

"You'd tell me if anything was wrong, wouldn't you?"

"Nothing's wrong, darling. Don't you worry your-self."

"But of course I worry. Grandpa, tell me, please."

"It's just a mood. It doesn't mean anything. When

a fellow gets to my age he starts having strange thoughts.''

''What kind of thoughts?'' Kaye asked in dismay. The mention of Bertie's age had brought old fears flooding back to her.

''I've been remembering Kedmore,'' Bertie said wistfully. ''It's nothing special, just a little village in the north. You won't even find it on most maps. But I was born and grew up there, and I'd kind of like to see it one more time—before it's too late.''

He finished with a small melancholy sigh. Sam, shamelessly eavesdropping behind a tree, made urgent signals to his partner-in-crime not to overdo it.

''Grandpa, what are you talking about?'' Kaye asked. ''It's not going to be 'too late' for a long time yet.''

''Of course it isn't,'' Bertie said bravely. ''Don't give it another thought.''

''I must think of it, if it's important to you. If you really want to see Kedmore again, why don't we take a little trip?''

''Oh, no, darling, I don't want to be a nuisance.''

''Don't say that. How could you ever be a nuisance to me? We'll go tomorrow.''

''Couldn't we go today?'' Bertie asked in a faint voice.

''But Jack will expect me here when he comes back—oh, yes, of course. Right now. I'll go and get ready.''

''Yes, hurry up. There's lots to get organized—packing, airline tickets—''

''Airline tickets?'' she echoed, puzzled. ''For Kedmore?''

"Oh, yes, right. Don't take any notice, darling. I'm just a bit distracted."

Kaye hurried upstairs and hurriedly packed for herself and Bertie. The two old men were standing in the hall when she went downstairs.

"All ready to go?" Bertie said eagerly. Kaye smiled at him, touched by his childlike delight.

"I just need a moment to leave Jack a note," she said.

"It'll soon be too late to start today," Bertie said. "And I did so want to go at once."

"No need to write to Jack," Sam said. "I'll explain what happened. Go on, you two."

As they were getting into the car, Sam asked, "Any idea when you'll be back?"

"Well..." Kaye looked at Bertie.

"Hard to say," he said vaguely. "You know how these things—see how it goes, eh?"

"I really don't know when we'll be back," Kaye said, laughing. "You'll explain to Jack, won't you?"

Sam's face was bland and innocent. "Don't worry, darling. I'll tell Jack everything he needs to know."

"I feel bad about leaving when he's coming home, but I've neglected Grandpa recently. Maybe the time has come to put him first. I'm sure Jack will understand."

"I'll see he does," Sam promised.

The last mile home seemed an eternity to Jack. He checked the huge bouquet of red roses on the passenger seat, his gift to Kaye to signal their new beginning. He wasn't sure what to say to her, but with any luck there would be no need for words. The flowers carried their own message, and perhaps he could leave the rest to her.

He wondered now whether his proposal really *had* been a spur-of-the-moment decision? Hadn't question and answer been given all those years ago in the Caribbean?

His own voice came to him out of the past. *You'll find a man who knows how to treat you, and you'll love him. He'll be the luckiest man alive.* He'd said those words to her as she wept in anguish at his refusal to make love to her. They sounded like a conventional disclaimer. It was only now that he knew he'd meant them all along.

He stepped on the gas a little, eager to get back to her. She'd probably be waiting for him on the front step. She often watched for him from the window and hurried down to greet him. Strange how a little loving gesture like that could come to mean so much, and how long it could take a man to understand.

He was several hours behind schedule, owing to a delay with Georgy's plane, and it was late evening when he reached home. He strode into the house, bouquet in hand, calling, "Kaye!" in the eager voice that had always brought her running down to him before. But this time there was only silence, and something in the echoing quality of the house made him uneasy.

"Kaye!" he called again.

When there was no response he ran through the house, still calling. He stopped in the back room overlooking the garden. It was a room Kaye had made her own, and now it seemed ominously quiet.

"I'm glad you've come back, son."

Jack turned quickly to find Sam in the doorway, his face troubled.

"Sam, where's Kaye?"

"I don't know," Sam said heavily. "I wish I did."

"What does that mean?"

"She left hours ago."

"What do you mean, 'left'?"

"She and Bertie just piled their stuff into the car and drove off."

"But where were they going?"

Sam crossed his fingers behind his back. "They were a bit cagey about that."

"Sam, what's going on here?"

"There's a lot going on that I don't understand," Sam said. "I thought you might know. Kaye's your wife. Don't you ever talk to her?"

"Of course we talk," Jack said, a tad defensively. "It's just that recently—she's been in a funny mood."

"I've noticed that, too," Sam said, adding significantly, "And now she's gone."

Jack tried to fight down his growing alarm. "When is she coming back?"

"I asked her that. She said she really couldn't say."

Jack's fingers tensed on the stems of the roses. "Didn't she leave me a note?"

Sam shook his head. "Not even that," he said heavily. "But she said you'd understand that the time had come."

"What the hell does that mean?" Jack demanded, raising his voice to drown out the sound of his own dread.

"I know she's been very depressed now that you don't want her anymore."

"Who says I don't want her?" Jack roared.

"You did—good as."

"What the hell are you talking about?"

"Let's face it, she's served her purpose," Sam said belligerently. "Got rid of Elsie for you. Now you don't need her anymore. Leastways, that's what she thinks."

"How could she think…?" Jack's voice trailed off, leaving him staring into space. A cold hand was gripping his stomach and he had the feeling of moving through a nightmare.

He forced his limbs into life and bounded up the stairs. In Kaye's room he pulled open closets and drawers. Most of her things were still there, but this didn't reassure him. He knew his wife well enough by now to understand that possessions meant very little to her. If she'd left him, she was more likely to have abandoned everything than to have stripped the place.

"She must have given you some idea," he said fiercely to Sam, who'd followed him.

"All I know is, I heard them talking about airline tickets," Sam said truthfully.

Jack went pale and walked out. He needed to be alone to cope with his thoughts. Kaye had always been completely his, there when he wanted her, wanting nothing for herself, only to make him happy. Now she was no longer there, and suddenly he was shaking.

In the kitchen Sam was staring at the phone on the wall, silently willing it to ring. When it did he snatched it up.

"Where in thunder have you been?" he demanded without preamble.

"Kedmore," came Bertie's voice. "Cornfield Guest House."

"Well, you took your time calling."

"I had to wait until Kaye went upstairs. She's asleep now."

"You don't know what you've put me through. I've got him all fevered up and I don't know where to send him."

"Well, you know now, so quit yakking and get up here," Bertie told him. "And hurry. Kaye's set on starting for home tomorrow."

"Don't let her leave till we get there," Sam yelped.

"I'm doing my best. Get moving!"

"Heck, I think I can hear Jack coming."

"Then I'm off. He's the last person I want to talk to." Bertie hung up.

Sam replaced the receiver just as Jack looked in.

"Who was that?"

"That old idiot Bertie!"

"Why didn't you call me?" Jack demanded.

"Didn't have the chance. He said you were the last person he wanted to talk to."

"What about Kaye?"

"She's asleep. But I found out where they are." Sam gave the name and location of the guest house, adding, "He used to live in Kedmore. Must have wanted to see his old home again before leaving the country."

"He *said* that?" Jack demanded.

"Not in so many words," Sam said truthfully. "But that was the impression I got."

"Get a map, quickly."

"It's four hundred miles north. Bertie's mentioned that place before."

"Can we do it by morning?"

"We can if we share the driving. Let's get going."

"I'm going to talk to her first."

"Maybe that's not a good idea…" Sam began nervously.

"Just get the car, Sam."

Sam departed, crossing his fingers.

He was in luck. The Cornfield was a tiny place with only three rooms and one telephone, and Bertie was prepared. When the call came through to reception he was lingering in the hall. "I'll take it," he said in answer to the landlady's query.

"Bertie, what the hell are you two doing up there?" Jack demanded in an edgy voice.

"Any reason why we shouldn't be?" Bertie responded with lofty dignity.

"Yes. Kaye's my wife. She should be at home." Jack hadn't meant it to come out quite as peremptory as it sounded, but he was too upset to be tactful.

"Jack, I don't know what's happened between you two, but that kind of attitude may be the reason Kaye decided to—well, it's none of my business."

"Too right. Put her on."

"I can't do that."

"Why the devil not?"

"She's asleep."

"So wake her," Jack snapped. The easy charm that had carried him through a thousand crises was deserting him now. This crisis was different. It mattered.

"I'm not waking her up at this hour," Bertie said firmly. "She's tired and—and not quite herself."

"What does that mean?"

Bertie chose his words carefully. "I've never seen her in this mood before. Of course, you never really know what Kaye's thinking."

Jack was about to say "Nonsense" when he remembered how often Kaye had surprised him. But never like this.

"Thinking about what?" he asked carefully.

"Well, she hasn't said much, but I know her better than anyone—a lot better than you do—and I've picked up signs you may have missed."

Jack ground his nails into his palm. "Will you come to the point?" he asked through gritted teeth.

"Would you say she's been happy?"

"Of course she—I've tried to make her happy— why should she...? What has she said?"

"Nothing specific," Bertie said, keeping just the right side of the truth. "But signs, you know. Why do you think she isn't at home now?"

"I'm waiting for someone to tell me that," Jack said, controlling himself with difficulty.

"And only Kaye could tell you."

"Then put her on."

"She'll talk to you when she's ready."

"You don't mean she's refusing?"

"I think I'd better not answer that question."

"Now, look here, Bertie, you get her to this phone. I mean it."

"Bye, Jack."

"Do you hear me?"

The line went dead.

"Not like you to holler at folks like that," Sam observed from the doorway. "Especially Kaye."

"I was talking to Bertie. He wouldn't put me through to her." He was too absorbed to notice Sam's quick sigh of relief. "He said—he implied—that she didn't want to talk to me." He raised horrified eyes to his father. "Dad—could that be true?"

"Could be. The sooner we get going the better."

Sam turned quickly out of the room to hide his smile. Jack hadn't called him Dad for years.

Sam took the first stint of driving, leaving Jack with nothing to do but brood. It was a horrid experience. When he couldn't bear it anymore he took over the wheel. But he couldn't concentrate, and at last Sam, swearing loudly, made him stop and move over.

"Get some sleep," Sam commanded. "You're going to need it."

He knew he wouldn't be able to sleep, but he rested his head on the back of the seat, closing his eyes.

The tooting of a horn woke him sharply. He sat up with a start, blinking against the daylight. His watch told him he'd slept for seven hours. The car was stranded in the middle of a flock of sheep.

He rubbed his eyes. "What the—?"

"Move 'em!" Sam was yelling to someone out of the window.

There was some backchat from a man Jack couldn't see, accompanied by baaing. Sheep milled around in all directions.

The shepherd put his head through the window. "Cars aren't supposed to come down this road," he explained.

"What's the use of saying that now?" Sam demanded. "We're here. Get us out!"

The shepherd gave him an affronted look and vanished.

"What time is it?" Jack demanded. "Nine? My God, they could have gone by now."

The sheep cleared at last and they were able to get up some speed. Jack ground his nails into his palms, wondering if he was going to lose the woman he loved because of a flock of sheep.

At last they reached Kedmore, a small village with one main street, lined with buildings that looked several hundred years old. Jack put his head out of the window and yelled desperately, "Cornfield Guest House—somebody—*please.*"

"Two hundred yards down on the left," shouted a man.

To their relief the sign for the Cornfield came into view almost at once. The first thing they saw was Kaye's car standing outside, and there was Kaye, piling luggage into the open trunk. Jack was out of his vehicle while it was still moving.

"Kaye!" he called hoarsely. *"Kaye!"*

She looked up in surprise. "Jack, I—"

Without waiting for her to finish, Jack seized her in his arms. "You shouldn't have done it," he cried. "Not without talking to me first."

"But I—"

"How could you just leave without a word? Don't you know that I can't live without you?"

His mouth was on hers before she could answer, kissing her fiercely as though he was trying to take her by storm without giving her time to think. Kaye was in a daze. Only the words *Don't you know that I can't live without you?* were real, and they lit up the sky.

She kissed him back eagerly, content to wait for explanations if only Jack would hold her in his arms and kiss her like this forever.

"I didn't know," he said when he could bear to free his lips. "I never dreamed how much I loved you until last night when Sam said you'd gone—"

"Sam—?"

"There are so many things I want to say to you, my darling, but I kept putting them off. I thought we had all the time in the world. If I'd guessed that you thought—never mind that. I love you, Kaye. I think I've loved you for years, and I know that I'll love you all my life. Come back and give me another chance. I can make it right this time. But don't leave me like this, I can't bear it."

Kaye regarded him in astonishment. How could he think she would ever leave him? But before she could speak she noticed Sam and Bertie, out of the corner of her eye. They were signaling frantically for her to keep quiet, and some hint of the truth dawned on her.

On second thoughts, she decided, maybe explanations could wait for another time. Just now she wanted to enjoy the bliss of hearing him say he loved her.

"I'll stay," she told him, "if you really want me to."

"I'm going to spend my life showing you how much I really want you. Come home with me, Kaye. Give me the chance to win your love. I need you very much."

"Win my love?" she echoed. "But I've always loved you. That was the only reason I married you."

He looked at her lovely face, only half believing her. It was still hard for him to accept a gift, and now the gift he was being offered was the one he wanted more than anything in the world.

"You once made me a promise," he reminded her. "Anything, any time, any place. You said yourself that you haven't redeemed it yet, so I'm calling it in now. What I want from you is this—everything, always, everywhere. And I'm never going to let you off the hook."

"You won't need to," she said joyfully. "I'm going to make that promise again, every day of our lives."

He took her hand and led her back into the guest house.

"We'd like the key again, please," he said to the landlady. "My wife's changed her mind. She'll be needing the room today, after all."

"Will I?" Kaye asked.

"Yes," he said firmly. "We will."

Sam and Bertie, happy to be forgotten, had been silent witnesses. As Kaye and Jack vanished up the stairs they exchanged looks of triumph. Then, as one man, they went to stand looking up at the windows.

"Which is hers?" Sam asked.

"The one with the chintz curtains," Bertie said.

"They've all got chintz curtains, you lamebrain!"

"*Those* chintz curtains—the ones that somebody is just closing."

They watched the male hands drawing the curtains firmly together, shutting out the world and enclosing the two within in a world of their own, where there was only happiness and fulfillment.

"I need a drink," Bertie said.

"So do I," Sam said with feeling. "Anywhere open this early?"

"Just down the road."

After a last triumphant look at the window they began to stroll off down the street.

"You were long enough coming," Bertie grumbled.

"Not my fault you were so late calling," Sam riposted. "And the journey—*sheep!* Trust you to have been born at the back of beyond."

"We did it!" Bertie said with satisfaction.

"We did it!"

Together they roared, *"Yes!"*

"Think they know?" Bertie asked as they resumed walking.

"Kaye knows. Jack doesn't, but that's because he's a fool."

"Like his dad."

"Do we find that pub soon, or do you just go on yakking forever...?"

* * * * *

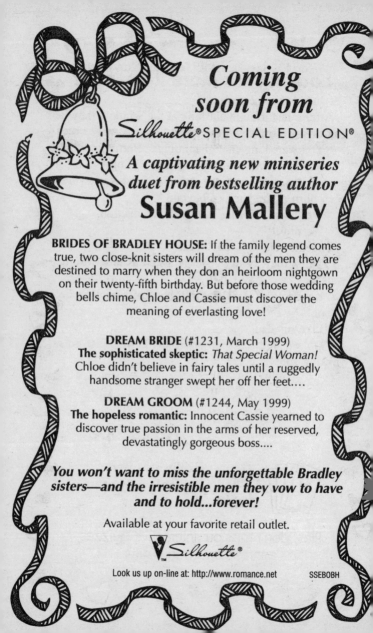

This March Silhouette is proud to present

SENSATIONAL

MAGGIE SHAYNE
BARBARA BOSWELL
SUSAN MALLERY
MARIE FERRARELLA

This is a special collection of four complete
novels for one low price, featuring a novel
from each line: Silhouette Intimate Moments,
Silhouette Desire, Silhouette Special Edition
and Silhouette Romance.

Available at your favorite retail outlet.

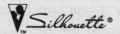

World's Most Eligible Bachelors

**Available March 1999 from
Silhouette Books...**

Doctor in Disguise
by Gina Wilkins

The World's Most Eligible Bachelor: Tall, dark and
devastating Dr. Alex Keating's cure for his chronic
bachelorhood: "Take" sexy Carly Fletcher and call
her in the morning!

One bump to the head left Dr. Alex Keating stranded
in the tender loving care of down-home physician
Carly Fletcher. She knew nothing of his stellar creden-
tials, but his long, lean physique and seductive smile
were all she *needed* to know to write this stubborn
patient a prescription for love!

Each month, Silhouette Books brings you a
brand-new story about an absolutely irre-
sistible bachelor. Find out how the sexiest,
most sought-after men are finally caught.

Available at your favorite retail outlet.

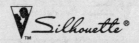

Based on the bestselling miniseries

FORTUNE'S *Children* ™

A FORTUNE'S CHILDREN *Wedding:*
THE HOODWINKED BRIDE

by BARBARA BOSWELL

This March, the Fortune family discovers a twenty-six-year-old secret—beautiful Angelica Carroll *Fortune!* Kate Fortune hires Flynt Corrigan to protect the newest Fortune, and this jaded investigator soon finds this his most tantalizing—and tormenting—assignment to date....

Barbara Boswell's single title is just one of the captivating romances in Silhouette's exciting new miniseries, **Fortune's Children: The Brides,** featuring six special women who perpetuate a family legacy that is greater than mere riches!

Look for *The Honor Bound Groom,* by Jennifer Greene, when **Fortune's Children: The Brides** launches in Silhouette Desire in January 1999!

Available at your favorite retail outlet.

Silhouette ®

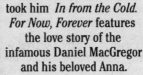

#1231 DREAM BRIDE—Susan Mallery
That Special Woman!/Brides of Bradley House
According to family legend, Chloe Wright was destined to dream of her future husband on her twenty-fifth birthday. The self-proclaimed pragmatist didn't believe in fairy tales…until enigmatic Arizona Smith mysteriously entered Chloe's life—and passionately swept her off her feet.

#1232 THE PERFECT NEIGHBOR—Nora Roberts
The MacGregors
Brooding loner Preston McQuinn was determined never to love again. But he could hardly resist his vivacious neighbor Cybil Campbell, who was determined to win his stubborn heart. Would the matchmaking Daniel MacGregor see his granddaughter happily married to the man she adored?

#1233 HUSBAND IN TRAINING—Christine Rimmer
Nick DeSalvo wanted to trade in his bachelor ways for his very own family. And who better than Jenny Brown—his best friend's nurturing widow—to give him lessons on how to be a model husband? But how long would it take the smitten, reformed heartbreaker to realize he wanted *Jenny* as his wife?

#1234 THE COWBOY AND HIS WAYWARD BRIDE—Sherryl Woods
And Baby Makes Three: The Next Generation
Rancher Harlan Patrick Adams was fit to be tied! The only woman who'd ever mattered to him had secretly given birth to *his* baby girl. And he couldn't bear to be apart from his family for another second. Could the driven father convince fiercely independent Laurie Jensen to be his bride?

#1235 MARRYING AN OLDER MAN—Arlene James
She was young, innocent and madly in love with her much older boss. Trouble was, no matter how much Caroline Moncton enticed him, gorgeous cowboy Jesse Wagner insisted she'd set her sights on the wrong guy. But she refused to quit tempting this hardheaded man down the wedding aisle!

#1236 A HERO AT HEART—Ann Howard White
When Nathan Garner returned to Thunder Ridge, Georgia, he was enveloped in bittersweet memories of Rachel Holcomb. Walking away from her gentle tenderness hadn't been easy, but it had been necessary. Could he reclaim Rachel's wary heart—and bring his beloved back into his waiting arms?